TRUSTING THE ROCK STAR

SMALL TOWN DESIRES

MISSY WALKER

For my own rockstar B. Let's keep playing to the beat of our own drum… forever.

1

KIT

Autographs, fucking autographs.

I nodded to Jonesy, my trusted security, who knew exactly what to do.

He waved off the remaining crowd that surrounded us. We'd performed our latest hit, snaked our way to the bar, and signed countless tits and limbs at the airport before we'd even arrived here.

I needed another drink.

Jamie and Ryan were one step ahead of me, already hurling back their whiskeys in record fashion in the section they'd roped off for us.

"Fellas, give me the bottle."

Jamie passed the bottle of Jack, and I took a full swig, pretending not to notice the look Ryan gave me as it burned the back of my throat. I sunk into the velvet armchair with an unobstructed view of the stage.

She sat on her stool, uncomfortable as a big toe in small sneakers with wild red hair flowing down to her slim waist. She sang—check that, strangled cats sounded better than whatever came out of those lips. Her hair blazed under the spotlights as she read the words on the screen, her body rigid, and her face burned brighter with each second that passed.

"They sound like shit." Jamie chuckled, following my gaze.

"The two at the front are all right, but the redhead sounds like me after touring nonstop for a year," I replied, my gaze unwavering in its curiosity.

"Is that who it is?" Ryan asked, laughing. "She sounds like nails down a chalkboard."

"Give her some free singing lessons, Kit. I saw you staring at her from the stage." Jamie winked.

"I'd like to school her in the art of fellatio." It had been a while since I had a bird's eye view of a redhead, but something about her made me doubt she was into the groupie thing."

"I've got my eye on the blonde who's been eye-fucking me ever since we walked through the door." Jamie stared at the bar where said blonde was. He lifted his hand to signal her to join us where we sat and nodded to Jonesy, who waved her through the cordoned-off area.

Jamie didn't need to be in the group to get laid. His perfect facial hair, thick black curls, and olive skin—a nod to his Greek heritage—had women fawning over him.

"Hiya, Kit, I'm Kiera." A petite girl with a pushup bra walked in front of me, lowering her seductive gaze.

"Hey, babe, come on over here," Jamie patted his knee, signaling for her to sit there.

"Hey," I nodded, returning my attention to the peculiar sound coming from the redhead on stage.

Why? I have no idea, but she still held my attention. Probably because out of everyone here, she ignored me, glaring at her phone during our impromptu performance. She stared at that thing, not remotely interested that we were in this dead-end town and in her bar. Not singing along, like the two women she was with and everyone else in the venue that had clearly exceeded its capacity limit.

I puffed out my cheeks. Well, she was tone-deaf and awkward as fuck. I took another swig of Jack, but it did nothing to ease the frustration brewing in my veins.

"These are my friends, Annabelle and Claudine," Kiera said, interlacing her fingers with two other gorgeous women who were definitely up for blowing us. So what else was new?

"Hey," I said as the brunette sat beside me, her leg purposely grazing mine.

She held out her hand. "I'm Claudine."

Of course, you are.

"What's up?"

"So you boys must be tired if you just got off a flight?" Claudine asked, blinking her caked-on mascaraed eyes at me.

"Very." The alcohol we drank from the airport was slowly losing its buzz.

"There must be a bed nearby?" She smiled, tilting her head to the side.

She had a nice rack.

So did the firecracker on stage.

She continued, "Anyway, are you on vacation?"

I didn't answer. Instead, my attention pulled back to the stage, hearing Ryan answer for me.

Vacation? That word was nonexistent. We hadn't taken a break since we burst onto the scene after high school. And for the next three weeks, we were stuck in this dead-beat town to lay down an EP in a remote cottage. And by cottage, I meant mansion. Our record label, Parallel Records, booked the sweet house, but under one condition

—get out of Manhattan, stop the partying and boozing so that we could clean up our tattered image.

I hadn't been back home to Australia since forming the band out of school seven years ago. Even when I felt suffocated to the point I had to come back, I didn't. I couldn't.

In all that time, I hadn't seen my parents either. They didn't like to fly, so they hadn't come to New York to visit. In fact, they hadn't been outside of Australia ever. But talking regularly via video calls seemed to satisfy them.

Just being back in the country for a mere few hours had tipped me over to the point of needing a drink or eight.

Sporadic applause echoed around the room as the stage lights haloed the crowd. She stepped off stage quicker than her friends. Wearing a knee-length dress and a slash of cherry red on her lips, she was the hottest yet most understated beauty in the club.

I walked over to the bar and called the bartender. "Margarita and a whiskey, neat."

"Sure thing, Kit," he replied.

"Margarita? How did you know I like those?" Claudine pursed her lips together.

Where the fuck did she come from? Had she followed me?

"Make it two margaritas," I held up two fingers, and he nodded.

I winked at her. *God, was she even legal?* That's all I needed.

Kit Found Fornicating with Underage Girl… Her Parents Sue. I could just see the headline now.

Fuck me. I had enough to deal with.

"How old are you, sugar?"

"Turned nineteen this week." She slid her hand up my thigh. "Maybe we should go somewhere?" She twisted her plump lips, her overpowering perfume invading my nostrils.

"Should we?" I love to hate groupies. This one was no exception.

"On the house, Kit." The bartender placed the three drinks on the wooden bar.

"Cheers, my man."

"Would you mind signing this? My girlfriend will shoot me if I don't at least try." He slid me a napkin and pen, a sheepish smile set across his face.

"For sure." I laughed, taking the napkin and signed my autograph like I had millions of times before.

"I'll do you one better. Leave your details with Clyde, my bouncer, and I'll organize some signed merch." I looked over at Clyde, who nodded that he'd heard me.

"No way! Man, that's sweet. Thanks so much."

"Sure thing."

"That is so sweet of you, Kit." She purred out, her pointy nails running down the curves of my shoulder.

I handed her the rounded glass, then signaled the boys. "I'll be back in a bit."

Ryan acknowledged me with a tilt of his head.

"Hey, where are you going?" She whined like I imagined a nagging wife would.

I grabbed my tumbler and cocktail and headed to the stage. At the risk of sounding like Arnold Schwarzenegger —but still not giving a shit—I replied, "I'll be back."

Between back slaps and compliments such as, "Hey, man, you rock!" and, "Kit, can I have your babies?"

Jonesy had cleared enough of a path to get me close to her.

She sat, back straight and perfectly poised, a few steps ahead of me. Her face was porcelain white with green-speckled eyes popped against the fire-auburn hair that tumbled down her back.

"I got this, Jonesy. Thanks, bud."

Slowly, she turned her head. A tiny crease appeared on her forehead as her gaze landed on mine.

The short blonde girl in a top with shiny little discs on them stood. "Kit, hi. I'm Lily."

I tipped my chin and smiled. "Hey, Lily."

She continued, "This is Amber, and this is—"

"Jazzie…" I breathed out in a low voice, completing her sentence and cutting her off.

"Ah, it's Jasmine. And how do you know my name?" One of her eyebrows perched higher than the other, her eyes narrowing at me, shortening her name.

I shrugged it off. "The DJ. He read out your names, and if that's Lily and that's Amber…" I trailed off.

"Right." She deadpanned.

I held up the glass in my hand. "Margarita?"

"No thanks," she snapped, her tone clipped.

Well, fuck, this is new. I glanced at Lily and Amber for some clue as to why this firecracker had a stick of dynamite up her pipe hole.

"She would love it," Amber smiled, quickly taking it from my hands and setting it down on the table in front of Jazzie. Jasmine. *Whatever.*

"Sit, please," Amber suggested.

I sat on the seat next to Jazzie. *Why didn't she take the drink? It's not like I'd roofie her. Shit, I was Kit Jones. Grammy Award Winner, slayer of women, playboy of Manhattan.*

Well, that was my public persona.

"Are you guys back in town for a tour?" Lily asked.

"Nah, we're recording a new track in Seaview. Only here for three weeks, then straight back to New York."

"You're in Seaview for three weeks? Why here and not the city?" Amber asked.

She was right, Brisbane, the main city, was only an hour away, but the record company insisted on a quieter town where we couldn't get into trouble. *Ha,* little do the fuckers know we're here, drunk and ready to party.

"There's a studio in Seaview which is perfect for the job. It's quiet, out of the way, without any distractions."

My eyes narrowed toward Jasmine, who again seemed more interested in her fucking phone than me. "So, Jasmine, that's quite a voice you got there."

She put her phone down and glared at me with her piercing emeralds.

"If that's your attempt at being nice, I think you should go back to your groupies."

A bark of laughter left my mouth. What else could I do?

Was she serious?

Lily pointed an arsenic-laced stare toward Jasmine. "Sorry about my friend. She's had a rough week."

Jasmine flicked her shiny hair behind her shoulder, cornering my attention. "I guess what I'm saying is not all of us have voices like yours, Kit. It is Kit, isn't it?"

It is Kit? What the fuck? The vein in my neck throbbed while simultaneously, my dick twitched. It was a weird feeling to be confronted with.

"Yeah, it's Kit."

"What kind of name is that, anyway?" She shifted in her seat, and the slit of her flowing dress slipped apart, exposing her creamy long legs.

Fuck, how I'd love to run my fingers up her creamy thigh and into her wet folds. She was fucking gorgeous, and she either knew it or had zero clue of her effect on me.

"Don't know. You'd have to ask my folks." I sipped my drink, enjoying the back and forth.

Amber laughed. "That could be arranged."

Jazzie shot her bullets, and Amber's laughter dissolved into silence.

A thought tipped my mouth upward into a grin. "It could. They're actually not too far away."

Now I had Lily and Amber's attention. Maybe Jasmine would get on board. "We could ask them tonight. I've got a driver with a dividing screen." I winked at Jasmine. "We can drive there now." I threw back my whiskey, and it slid down my throat, dulling the noise.

"You're kidding, right?" Jasmine huffed, her little nostrils flaring the size of pecans.

"Nope." *Why would I joke about that?*

She shook her head. "You're on another planet."

"Jasmine!" Lily scolded her friend.

"Kit, if you think I'm just going to throw myself at you because you're some rock god, you picked the wrong girl."

"Is that right?" I asked, trying to ignore the throbbing vein.

"Yes. So I think you can take your margarita and give it to the blondie who's been eye-fucking you ever since you left her side."

Laughter echoed around us as I realized people were hovering like flies near the table. *Were they laughing* at *me?*

She turned toward her friends, who appeared as taken aback as me. Except, I wore my mask well. Years of being in the spotlight can do that to a man.

It wasn't my intention to be rude or indignant. *Screw you, princess.*

I laughed with the others that had gathered around. Hell, no skin off my back. The redhead rejected me in front of a crowd. Never in the history of rock stars had that ever happened.

To avoid saying something I shouldn't, I turned around and stalked off, knowing exactly where I was headed. My hands balled into fists at my side, my restraint barely there.

"Another whiskey, neat, Kit?" the bartender asked as I marched up to the bar, flinging my hands over the bar mat.

"Make it a double." I shifted my attention to the blondie back in the corner. "Hey."

Her face illuminated like she'd won the meat raffle at the local bingo meet. "Yes, Kit?" She purred, siding up to me and batting her eyes.

The bartender poured my drink. *Double?* It was more like a triple. I drank it in one gulp, slamming the empty glass on the counter, and sucked in a well-needed breath.

I fished out a bill from my back pocket. "Thanks, bud," I said and slapped it into his hand. "That's for you, friend."

He looked at the bill, then up at me, eyes the size of saucers. "Kit, that's generous, man. Thanks so much."

"Pleasure." I smiled. Turning, I reached for the groupie's hand. "Come with me," I commanded, needing to release the throbbing Jazzie put between my legs.

As I rushed through the crowd, my head started spinning, and my focus shifted as I went past dresses and flashes of colors. Finally, I saw an opening on the side of the wall and headed toward it. Two doors appeared in front of me. Fifty-fifty odds weren't that bad. I opened the door and found somewhere to lean on.

She stood in front of me and knew exactly what to do.

After she dropped to her knees, she undid my zipper, then started taking to it like it was her favorite ice cream. I put my hands on the back of her head and guided her deeper.

The more her lips glided up and down my shaft, the harder I got. Not because of her. It was the idea of being turned down that got me off. The image of the flame-haired vixen who rejected me was getting me harder by the second.

"What the fuck?" A woman's voice echoed in the bathroom, bouncing off the tiles and hitting me square in the chest.

Fuck. Obviously, fifty-fifty odds weren't good enough. I looked around—no urinals in here. *My bad.*

My attention shifted to the voice at the entrance. Her white dress, creamy skin, and narrowed eyes were just on my mind.

Jazzie.

"Fuck me," I groaned.

"Predictable," she muttered before turning on her heel.

I removed my cock from blondie's mouth and zipped myself up.

"Don't worry about her." Blondie clawed at my zipper, proudly putting the G in groupie.

There was no way I'd be getting off now. "Just go, sugar."

She got off her knees and sulked toward the exit, heels clicking against the hollow tiles.

I turned around and leaned on the vanity, staring at myself in the mirror. With both eyes bloodshot, wearing the same clothes for days, and waxy, unwashed hair that resembled an oil rag and smelled like gasoline, how was I voted in the top ten sexiest men alive?

Fucking ridiculous.

Running myself into the ground, hurting women like it was my favorite card game, and drinking it up had become a daily job. It was my only escape from the guilt that had consumed me since his death. If I didn't stop soon, the cliff that lay beneath me would desecrate, taking me with it.

The last few months, when I trended downward, my parents had tried to contact me more than usual, but I'd pushed them away.

They didn't even know I was back in the country. I

took out my phone, stared at the blank screen, then slid it back into my pocket. I couldn't tell them yet.

What would Drew say about that? He'd be turning in his fucking grave.

I wish I could join him. Or take his place.

What I would give to take his place.

I just wanted the pain to stop.

2

JASMINE

My head hurt, but I wasn't hungover.

Thank the stars it was Friday. My date for the weekend—anything on Netflix and a bottle of red. Hiking with Lily could wait. I just wanted to chill and catch up on sleep.

"Jasmine, let's gooo!" Amber yelled from the kitchen. God knows why, when she could speak at a normal decibel, and it still would have the same effect. Our two-bedroom apartment in Seaview was a non-insulated shoebox—an icebox in winter and a sweat box in summer, like Bikram Yoga Hot.

Living opposite the beach came with sacrifices. And to pay minimal rent, we sacrificed the size of our apartment. Still, it was our home, and if I continued to pay my share of the rent, it would remain home.

"Holy Toledo, girl. Kim Kardashian is quicker than you."

I shoved one foot, then the other, into my Converse high-tops and shouldered my backpack. "I'm coming. Keep your panties on."

"Love the look. I wish I could get away with sneakers at work." Amber eyed me.

Casual was my style, and the fact I could get away with it at work was a bonus. Probably the only perk I'd ever get. Today, I picked lilac overalls and a white scoop-neck T-shirt.

We couldn't be more opposite. Her brown hair, sleek and shiny, was pulled into a tight bun. She stood against the floral armchair, wearing a black pencil skirt, silk blouse, and black stilettos. She could easily pass as a funeral director rather than a lawyer.

"My boss might be an ass, but at least he lets us wear whatever we like." I guess that was the local newspaper for you. Relaxed, yet competent.

Snatching the keys to my beat-up Volkswagen, I slammed the apartment door and turned the key so it clicked to lock.

I stepped outside, and the humidity hit me like a slap across the face.

"Ugh, it's stifling!" Amber groaned, pulling her blouse off her skin and puffing it full of air.

"I know. Good news is I have enough anti-frizz in my hair to ignite a fire."

Amber tipped her head back in laughter. Humidity was definitely not my friend, especially in February—one of the hottest months in Seaview. My thick red hair flung around untamed with the sea breeze that rode into shore.

"By the way, I still can't get over what you said to *the* Kit Jones last night."

Do we have to rehash this? Last night Amber and Lily were gobsmacked at how I'd turned him down. Even when I said I'd walked in on him getting a blow job, they took his side, reminding me I was his first choice. *What the hell?*

"Well, get over it," I snapped.

"The guy practically said he wanted to sleep with you, Jazzie. What better way to get over your ex, who cheated on you, might I add, than with a fuckin' international rock star."

She had a point. *Still…*

I flung open the creaky car door and started the engine. It roared and sputtered like I just threw two grand out the window rather than to the mechanic to get her fixed.

"Come on. You've got to admit he's damn sexy."

"Well, if tatts and greasy hair are your thing…" I let my voice hang in the air, momentarily contemplating a night of wild unattached sex with a stranger. Yeah, that wasn't me.

"… and muscles and a golden tan. Oh, then, there are those eyes that would temper chocolate," Amber added.

I giggled. It was true. The guy was eye candy, even for nuns.

"Then he had his junk in some groupie's mouth, remember?"

"That's *so* rock star." Amber chuckled.

"Predictable is what it is." I gripped the steering wheel, the memory of his searing brown eyes pulling an ache between my thighs.

"Well, your loss was someone else's gain."

"No loss at all," I pressed the accelerator, and the car lurched into gear, screeching down the one-way street.

"Watch out!" Amber yelled, automatically gripping the brace overhead.

I slammed on the brakes, barely missing an elderly woman who quickly stepped back onto the pedestrian crosswalk.

"Shit, sorry." I held my hand up, apologizing. The

woman shook her head, then glared at me like I was the horn-wearing devil himself.

As soon as she crossed, I pressed the accelerator, then made a hard right turn, finding a parking spot right in front of the *Brisbane Times*.

I flicked my wrist and checked the time. "See? Right on time."

"Except, now the granola in my belly is hovering very close to being projected onto your windshield."

"Sorry, Ambs. You okay?"

"I'll be all right. Will you have time for lunch today?" Slowly, she leaned forward, gathering her leather tote bag.

"Yeah, I should. Two morning meetings and a quick zoom before lunch. I'll text you." Clutching my Thule backpack, I was super careful to protect what was inside, even though it was outdated camera gear. To me, it was priceless and my livelihood.

Amber waved, then strutted across the road, her stilettos an extension of her long legs. The law firm that had hired her a year ago was conveniently located across from the paper where I worked. She was knocking at the door of completing her five-year law degree and was already tracking to graduate with honors. That was Amber, a typical striver, getting distinctions like free samples at a bakery.

We'd met in a statistics class in the first year at Providence University. She was studying law, and I was one semester into my accounting degree before I realized I'd rather stab myself in the eyeball with a blunt fork than work with numbers for the rest of my life.

I walked into the building, and it buzzed with ringing phones, idle chatter, and the tapping of keyboards. "Morning, Fred," I said, grabbing my cup of coffee from the brown-stained coffee machine in the makeshift kitchen, then followed inside his office. One day, they'd renovate the office. Until then, we had to put up with the paint peeling off walls, the musty smell of moldy ceilings, and stray cockroaches that lay hidden in the back of the coffee machine.

"Jasmine, I have something for you."

Here we go. The last time Fred said that I spent all day getting down and dirty photographing a sewer outlet. The newspaper was doing an investigative piece about illegal sewage dumps flowing into the pristine beaches on the Sunshine Coast. Getting up close and personal photographing a sewer outlet was what I called a shitty day.

Or, the time when our journalist, Harry, who I was always paired with, and I had to drive to a remote movie set eight hours away, only to get stood up by the A-list actor we were scheduled to interview because she had a cold. *Okay, fine, whatever.* But then, having to turn back immediately because work didn't have the budget to put us up in a hotel. *Ugh, fuck's sake.*

I shouldn't complain. I really shouldn't but work over the last few months was like a noose tightening around my neck. Fred had given me a job when no one else would. With my limited photography skills, he'd hired me on the spot after I'd walked in—a college dropout with a folder of landscape photographs I'd taken in my spare time. And he always remembered the favor he'd afforded me. Jazzie Winters was the go-to photographer for last-minute scoops and interstate travel.

"What is it, Fred?" I sipped on my bitter black coffee, trying to mask my disinterest.

He frowned, the deep lines on his face and emaciated frame making him look a lot older than his forty-five years.

"Hear me out first. There's a band called Four Fingers

who arrived in Seaview last night. Have you heard of them?"

I shivered, but I wasn't cold. "I think so," I said.

"You think so? They're number one in eleven countries. Christ, Jazzie, the Holy Pope has heard of them."

"Not sure if blasphemy and the Holy Pope should be used in the same sentence," I goaded him as I always did.

He rolled his eyes, ignoring me. "They are here for three weeks, and I want you to follow them around the entire time."

My stomach lurched into my throat, and this time it wasn't from the cockroach-infested coffee. "What?"

"They're recording for three weeks in Seaview at the Holmes Estate. You know, the mansion up on the hill?"

Hell yes, I know it. It's a magnificent grand old white home with shutters and bougainvillea, and it looks like something that should belong on the Italian Riviera and certainly not a small coastal town.

"I know the Holmes Estate, but I'm too busy. Can't Mary do it?"

"Mary's about to pop any day now." *Dammit. She was looking rather swollen. I pitied the girl with this humidity, especially after she showed me what it did to her ankles, or cankles, as she called them.*

"Well, there's Bec." I firmly set down my coffee cup, and black liquid splashed onto the plastic desk. He raked a hand through his thinning gray hair, then handed me the tissue box. "Rebecca is too new for something like this. I need you. You are the best photographer we have."

I wiped the spilled coffee, determined to get out of this somehow. "But I haven't finished the nursing home scoop," I lied.

"Nonsense. You finished that. I've got enough in there to go to print."

Fuck's sake.

"Now the thing is, they actually want someone to photograph their journey writing the EP to release. So it's not a point-and-shoot job. You will be up close and personal with the band."

I scowled into my coffee. "Great."

"You can check that foul temper of yours, too, and remember your bedside manner. These guys are heroes wherever they go. Worshiped from the ground up."

I let out a frustrated sigh. *Why was I being dealt with the shit stick again?*

He steepled his fingers together and leaned forward in his chair. "Look, I knew you wouldn't be jumping up and down, but I thought you'd have more excitement than a limp dick!"

I let out a laugh. "Egos. I'd be dealing with a bunch of egomaniacs. I hate egos." I chewed the lead pencil and googled away on the desktop Mac. "I just think you can find someone else better suited for the job, that's all. Can't I kindly refuse?"

He puffed out his hollow cheeks. "Jasmine, do this, and you can pick your next assignments from here on out, okay?"

Talk about dangling cheese in front of a mouse. Did I just hear him say I could pick my next assignments? If Kit-*rock star*-Jones was who I had to endure to choose my work from here on out, I was in. Kit probably wouldn't even remember last night and certainly not me.

"Fine. When do I start?"

A smile set across Fred's face. "Now. *Tout suite*! They're expecting you up at the cottage in thirty minutes." He handed me a black folder. "Here, take the brief. Everything you need is in there. We've struck a deal with their public relations team, who arranged the whole thing with the *Bris-*

bane Times. So we get exclusivity, and they get good **PR** for their new record."

"What if it's not good **PR**. What if they're a bunch of hopeless singers, drunk and high as rainbow kites?" Just for effect, I widened my eyes, my lashes scratching against my eyelids.

He shot up and shoved his pen above his ear, his jaw ticked with anger.

Too far?

"I don't know if it's that time of the month or if your ex is still fucking with your head, but drop the attitude. Unless you want to see who else is hiring self-taught photographers?"

Asswipe. Using that against me was getting old, but bringing up the ex, hell, that was low. I had to make this work. Running back home to Mom and Dad wasn't an option, especially when they'd paid for me to go to college and I'd dropped out. And, when my sister, Grace, was the successful one, they had only wanted the same for me.

I feigned a smile. "No, I'll do it."

"Of course, you will. Now go, try to enjoy yourself. This is a once-in-a-lifetime scoop, Jazzie. Others would kill to be in your shoes." *Yeah? Whoop-de-fucking-do.*

I left his office, then finishing off my burned and likely-infested coffee, I grabbed my camera kit and hurried down the front steps to the bustling street.

Sitting in my decade-old Volkswagen wedged between two SUVs, I slammed the horn with a flat palm, letting the pent-up frustration boil over. The momentary relief that washed over me quickly vanished when the curious stares of people passing by made me feel like the crazy redhead alone in her rusted-out car.

That noose, fuck, it was tighter than ever now. I breathed in, but as deep as I tried to inhale, it wasn't enough to replenish the air in my lungs. Maybe it would be okay. I could just keep my professional distance for three weeks. They'd be busy doing all their recording stuff or whatever they did, and I'd be a photographer in the background.

Yes, In the background.

Alone.

As always.

* * *

After I pressed the buzzer, announcing myself to the man on the other side, the grand black iron gates swung open a moment later. I shifted my car into gear, and it jerked forward suddenly.

I drove along the crushed pebble driveway, its arches and curves soft against the thick emerald lawns. The owner of the estate moved to Seaview over a decade ago. Supposedly, he was a retired musician with a state-of-the-art recording studio. He'd often host successful artists in his home and parties similar to *The Great Gatsby*.

I'd finally reached the end of the driveway and approached what looked like a mirage. Rendered white walls and arched windows billowed with purple flowers while Ferraris, Lamborghinis, and Mustangs lined the circular paved driveway. I barely had time to take it all in when a tall man with wiry features opened my car door. It scraped the bottom of the car when it creaked open, and I stared at it like it was about to unhinge itself. Heat scaled my neck at the thought of losing a car door in front of Kit's doorstep. "Miss Jasmine Winters, welcome."

"Hi… hello, yes." I cleared my throat, hoping my voice was in there somewhere. "Call me Jazzie," I offered him a weak smile, then lifted my backpack off the passenger seat and stepped out. My dungarees, white T-shirt, and Converse shoes now looked utterly ridiculous in a place like this.

"The band is inside. Please follow me."

I took a hesitant step forward. The place was grand. No, that was an understatement. The foyer itself was larger than our two-bedroom apartment. We walked past a marble staircase into the large living area that overlooked an enormous lap pool. Along the entire length of the pool, the house split into two wings. Circular arched windows offered the perfect view from inside to out and framed the luxurious pool that spilled over the infinity edge.

"Lovely, isn't it?"

"Ah-ha." My response was barely audible as I picked my chin up off the marble floor.

"I'm Gregory. If you need anything while you're here for the three weeks, I'm your man."

I shook his hand. "Thank you, Gregory, but I'm not staying here."

"Yes, but you'll be here every day. The kitchen will provide all meals, and use of the amenities is encouraged."

"Okay." In my head, I was doing backflips. This house would be my sanctuary for the next three weeks. Guaranteed their coffee would be better.

"Now, follow me. Your reporter friend is also here. Harry."

Oh fuck. It gets better.

That sneaky son-of-a-bitch boss, Fred, forgot to mention that little piece of the puzzle. Only twenty-four and highly accomplished, Harry was the *Brisbane Times'* leading investigative journalist. He wanted to work for *60 Minutes*. Which begged the question, why did Fred put him on this job and not Sally, who covered all things entertainment?

Clearly, the band's public relations team or record company had cut a fat check to the newspaper, therefore, demanded the best. Not that I thought I was the best photographer.

As Fred said, no one else was available.

Gregory led the way past marble-veined hallways, decorated guest suites with private ensuites, and paneled walls covered with cool modernist art with an Andy Warhol vibe. We stopped when we arrived at the enormous yet minimalist kitchen. The refrigerator was one of those fancy Sub-Zero types and took up an entire wall.

"Paula, this is Jasmine." Paula closed the refrigerator door and turned to walk toward me. Tall, needle-thin with high cheekbones, she looked more like a middle-aged runway model than a chef.

"Hi, call me Jazzie," I offered. I'm only used to my mother calling me Jasmine.

She smiled, and it reached her eyes. "Nice to meet you, Jazzie."

"Jazzie will be here for the three weeks photographing the band," Gregory explained.

"Do you have any dietary requirements, Jazzie?"

Come again?

"Ah no, not if you count chocolate as an essential." Laughter erupted from only me. So awkwardly, I cleared my throat. "No. No allergies or anything like that," I replied with a low-set voice.

"Great, we will serve lunch shortly,"

"Can't wait." Anything would be better than my regular cheese sandwich or the rare day I ate out, a sushi roll.

Paula moved swiftly around the kitchen. She torched something with a small blow torch. and the caramelized sugar scent made my stomach flip with happiness.

Damn, the coffee would definitely be better here. The thought made me smile.

Maybe this would be all right after all. I could deal with a petulant rock star and Harry, who really ought to have gotten the hint I wasn't interested years ago.

"So the place can be a bit of a maze if you aren't used to it. Just think of the house as a spine in the middle with two wings. Each wing accommodates six bedrooms and bathrooms. The spine houses the essential services… kitchen, living, pool table, and study," Gregory added.

"Since when did a pool table become essential?"

That got a laugh out of Gregory. "Well, not in our worlds, Jazzie."

We walked out of the kitchen and through the tiled outdoor area where the pool sat positioned amongst the architectural gardens and rock walls.

"Here is the enormous pool. Feel free to use it, as sometimes the band breaks for extended periods during the day."

Nice perk. Maybe I could take a swim on the job. Technically, I couldn't photograph the band if they weren't available unless they were swimming too. The image of Kit's sculptured body in wet swim shorts clinging to his thighs caught me by surprise.

"Can you see that shack?"

I blinked, taking in my surroundings once again. "If you mean that huge stone-walled structure that looks like a house, then yes."

He laughed a horsey laugh. "That's the one. That is the studio. Sir Wallace calls it Amalia."

"Amalia?" I breathed out in a whisper.

"Rumor has it he named it after the one who got away… his first love."

"Oh."

"They're there now, recording and writing. It's best to enter quietly as the band doesn't like to be disturbed when in the flow."

"Sure."

We walked to the front door, and Gregory paused with his hand on the knob. "You don't seem like the type of girl to get star-struck," he said.

I shrugged. "They're just people."

He tilted his head. "That they are, Miss Jasmine. That they are."

"Jazzie, please," I insisted.

He opened the door, and my heart unexpectedly thundered in my chest.

3

———

KIT

Why did I drink last night?

Jetlag dragged like a motherfucker, and now Jamie and Ryan were teaming up on me like a bad porno. At least Angus, who'd flown in before sunrise, was shoving back the coffees rather than double-teaming me.

"So why didn't you bring back the hot blonde you had draped over you, Kit," Jamie inquired, downing his espresso and smirking at Ryan.

So they both got laid. *Big fucking congrats to you both.* I saw or rather heard their dates leave the house, quiet as fucking elephants, stomping out. Luckily, I was already up. "Didn't I?" I replied, not at all bothered by Jamie's taunting smirk.

"No, you didn't. Couldn't get it up, Kit?" Jamie grinned.

I rolled my eyes. "Maybe one day you'll get more pussy than me, Jamie."

"I did last night." He shot back quickly, and Ryan let out a laugh.

"Can't my dick get a day off? Or do you want some of

25

this?" I grabbed my junk, stood, and leaned in so I was up in his space.

"Fuck off, Kit." Jamie put his elbow up, shielding his face.

"Yeah, I thought so." I laughed, flopping back down on my studio chair.

"Who's Mr. Cranky Pants this morning? You know, getting laid takes the edge off, Kit. But I don't need to tell you that." Ryan picked up his midnight blue Fender Strat from the rack. He didn't need his irresistible charm to bed the ladies. His arsenal of baby blues, floppy blond locks, and a tongue ring did it with ease.

Getting laid would take the edge off for a minute, then what?

"Enough foreplay, let's play," I stood and shouldered my guitar, shutting down the conversation.

It was already midday when we'd run some lyrics. Well, *I'd* come up with the lyrics while Ryan and Jamie experimented with a few riffs and beats. That's how we worked best anyway. They took care of the musicality portion, and I handled the words that made the song.

My head pounded louder than a kick drum. I wanted to call it a day but knew it was out of the question. I'd push through like I always did.

At least the place was cool—relaxed and quiet, like rehab but without the high fence. A stint last year in New York's finest rehab facility saved me from spiraling headfirst into alcohol addiction. If it weren't for my willpower, I'd still be there. But that same willpower seemed to be wayward of late, and my publicist and record label were now suddenly heavily invested in my well-being. So they'd shipped me off, back to Australia, a place I'd avoided all this time and for a good reason.

"Hey, who hired the farmhand?" Jamie looked past me to the studio entrance.

"Sorry for the interruption, but may I introduce Jasmine from the *Brisbane Times* newspaper?"

Jasmine?

I swiveled on my seat, turning slightly. In my peripheral vision, I saw the same fiery red hair as last night.

Her face was the one I had in my dreams when I'd finally fallen asleep. Flawless porcelain skin and green eyes that saw straight through me were now staring at me from across the matted studio floor.

"What are you doing here?" Her relaxed posture had coiled into a ball of stiffness at my question. *Did she not think I'd remember her?*

"I'm here on a photography assignment for the next three weeks to capture you recording your song."

"It's an EP, love," Jamie scoffed, and I shot him a shut-the-fuck-up glare.

"You're a photographer?" I asked.

"I am." She pursed her lips together, and the same defiance she'd shown me last night burned brightly behind her green-flecked eyes once again.

My dick twinged in my jeans. What was it with this girl that had my dick on high alert?

"You two know each other?" Ryan asked, looking between us.

"Jasmine performed at the karaoke bar after we got offstage." I left out the part where she'd walked in on me with my junk in a groupie, another low point to add to my personal tally of never-ending disappointments.

"Performed, is that what you call it?" Ryan laughed, and I couldn't help but grin.

She narrowed her eyes at Ryan, then straightened. "I guess we can't all be rock stars."

Well, fuck. I knew there was something about her.

"So you've met our resident charmer, Ryan." I stared at her and smiled while feeling a spray of Ryan's bullets aimed toward me.

"That's Jamie." I gestured with a tip of my head in his direction.

"Hey, Jasmine." Jamie extended his hand, and she shook it. Son-of-a-bitch got to touch her milky white skin before me.

I cleared my throat. "And Angus, he's over there."

"Hey," he offered, waving his drumstick.

"I'll leave you, Mr. Jones." Gregory stepped back toward the door.

"It's Kit, Greg."

"Sorry. *Kit.*" He gave a sheepish smile.

Jasmine turned around to face Greg, and he shot her a reassuring smile. Surely, with all that bravado, she wasn't nervous?

The door creaked open, and Cohen stepped out from the control room. "Jasmine, I'm Cohen, the producer for Four Fingers. Why don't you come back here behind the glass? Harry is back here too."

Harry smiled at Jasmine through the glass. His perfect teeth, boring clothes, and overachieving attitude irked me even with a pane of glass between us. Harry already had twenty minutes with the guys and me this morning and saved the most intrusive questions for me. Apparently, he was the hotshot reporter our public relations company had hired. Already, I didn't particularly appreciate where he was coming from, and if he weren't careful, I'd have him thrown out of the estate. Although I wondered how much clout I had left to make those decisions now that the label had essentially said I was on my last warning.

"Sure thing, Cohen." She walked past me, and briefly,

our eyes met. Something swirled between us, thick and heady it squeezed the air from my lungs. She diverted her gaze quickly to something else behind me, making me wonder if she had felt it too.

No pane of glass could stifle whatever the fuck that was.

She must be damn good at what she did. Otherwise, she wouldn't be here. The label would have spared no expense for the best.

"Right, where were we, boys?" I tried to ignore the redhead sitting a few feet behind me in her short overalls and white Converse, the same pair of high tops I owned.

"Try an A-flat here, after the bridge," Jamie suggested.

"All right, let's try that. Three, two, one." I grabbed the mic and began losing myself in the song.

Even though we were rehearsing, I belted out the lyrics like I was in Madison Square Garden. Then, I opened my eyes, having forgotten I was in Seaview and not in front of tens of thousands of screaming fans. "All right, hold up," I said.

"Hey, man, that sounded wicked. Why'd you stop?" Jamie asked, confusion stretching across his face.

"It needs work," I replied flatly.

"Seriously? Which part?" Ryan questioned, looking equally perplexed.

"All of it," I snapped. Both Jamie and Ryan exchanged glances.

"Is it the four-four in the bridge?" Angus asked, sweating like he'd gone twelve rounds in a boxing ring. We all knew it wasn't from the coffee. Angus was known in the group to have a bit of a drug habit. *Whatever.* As long as he kept it in check, I didn't care what the fuck he got up to. The record company hired Angus, and at the time, he felt like a good fit for the band when we came to New York seven years ago. But now, I wasn't so sure.

"How's this?" He kicked a beat on the kick drum. It sounded all right. Just not perfect. It needed to be perfect. I wouldn't settle for anything less than perfection.

I held up my hand. "Let's just take a break, fellas." The truth was, I wanted to know more about the redhead drilling a hole into my back with her laser greens than working on a beat.

"Lunch, everyone," Gregory announced, and the timing could not have been any better.

Jamie turned to Gregory. "Did you call in the prosciutto?"

"Don't be a needy fuck, Jamie." The day we turned into a bunch of spoiled pricks with petty demands was the day we needed to walk away from each other. Her laughter filtered through to the studio. Although soft, I still heard it. Neither forced nor contrived, it reverberated down the length of my spine, touching my toes.

Jamie looked past me into the glass booth, presumably at her.

"What's funny?"

I turned around. Jazzie's eyes darted from Jamie to me. He put Jazzie on the spot, and curiosity got the better of me. I bit the inside of my cheek to stop myself from smiling.

"Well," she said evenly, pausing to choose her next words.

"Well... what?" Jamie demanded impatiently.

"Leave her alone, Jamie."

He puffed out his cheeks, then set his guitar down. His narrowed glare darted from Jasmine to me before he strode out with a heavy foot outside the studio.

It wasn't easy to get under Jamie's skin, but she had done it. I grinned, and her perfect mouth rose into a slight smile, digging her teeth into her bottom lip in an attempt to keep a straight face.

* * *

Lunch was delicious. I don't know why Jamie was so goddamn fussy, requesting this and that wherever we went. Honestly, it drove me mad.

Maybe I shouldn't have been so resistant to coming here. Perhaps the cottage would be the sprawling escape I needed. Drew would have loved everything about this place. Organic, local food prepared by an Australian Italian chef who was positively out of this world. I'd already finished my slow-cooked lamb and was now enjoying the creamy buffalo mozzarella salad with fresh Marzano tomatoes. I'd only known the name because Paula, our chef, happily recited what we were eating when she'd served it. Like music was inside of me, food was Paula's muse. You could tell the way her face beamed when she spoke of the food she'd prepared for us.

"All right, reset in fifteen minutes." Cohen finished the rest of his soda, then pushed out his chair to stand.

Our mastermind of a producer had been with us since we became overnight sensations. Based in New York with us, he'd produced all five of our albums. But more than that, Cohen had become more of a mentor to me, especially over this last year, than I'd probably care to admit.

The patio area was charming, even romantic if you were into romance. From here, you could see each sleeping wing. We'd only occupied five of the rooms but split up between the wings and had given Cohen the master suite considering his wife might fly out and join him toward the tail end of the trip.

Steel archways and white walls framed the hallways,

and from the outside, sprawling wisteria and bougainvillea colored the archways. I'd overheard Gregory comment on the names of the flowers earlier to Cohen. Protected from the searing summer sun, a hardwood framed patio fitted with automatic water misters sheltered our outdoor table. Sheeted with purple and pink flowering vines, it was like something out of a Henry James novel.

Her long hair blew in the warm breeze where she sat next to Harry, whose patches of sweat dampened his preppy boy white shirt and tie.

By the way she poked at her food, she seemed as interested in Harry as a supermodel was to carbs.

I hung back, watching as Jamie, Ryan, and Angus left. Moments after, Cohen followed, leaving only Jasmine, Harry, and me at the table. I waited to see if she, too, would linger.

I stared at Harry, who hung around longer than a groupie.

Off you go, jerk, back to the studio. No more journalistic-style questions for now. No more questions about going off the rails and sleeping with everyone in Manhattan.

He rose slowly and slid his chair underneath the table. Finally, he reached for his fanny pack or whatever it was he carried and turned to Jasmine.

"You coming, Jazzie?" Harry asked, turning around and arching a brow.

I stabbed my fork into the meringue on my plate. Why did *he* call *her* Jazzie?

Wasn't that just reserved for her friends? *Had Harry and Jazzie fucked?*

Unsure why I actually gave two fucks, I shook my head, trying to level out my thoughts.

"Yes, in my own time," she replied, holding her own. I smiled into my drink. *Damn firecracker.* Harry set off toward the studio. The guy even walked weirdly—hands stuck to the sides of his body and short but quick strides. It was like he had a carrot up his ass.

The clang of Jasmine arranging the cutlery on her plate steeled my attention. Then after a moment, she stood up before glancing in my direction.

"Jasmine?" I called out to her.

"Yes?" She flung her red hair over her shoulder to hang down her back, waves and all.

"Wait up. I'll walk back with you." I pushed my chair out, and it dragged on the tiles.

"I know the way," she huffed out.

"I know you know the way," I replied, but she'd already walked around the table, heading for the studio when I'd caught up. Jeez, stubborn? That was an understatement.

We walked side by side, and I wasn't sure if it was the myriad of flowering gardens or her perfume that smelled almost edible. I turned to her, imagining laying her down in the field, legs splayed, and eating her out until she screamed my name in waves of multiple orgasms.

"So I guess I should apologize for…" I scratched at my stubble.

"Me walking in on you getting a blow job?"

"Yeah, that."

"You ought to be more careful where you get off," she said as if she'd just commented on the weather rather than my junk.

"I was drunk."

"And…"

"Well, when I'm drunk, I do stupid shit."

"Like invite me to meet your parents in the middle of the night so we could have sex in the back of a limo?"

"Did I tell you it had one of those dividing screens?" I winked and pressed my lips together, anticipating her response. She smiled, then just as quickly as it appeared across her face, it vanished, replaced with a frown.

"You can't blame a guy for trying, can you?"

She said nothing, and I had this innate urge to tell her nothing had happened. "Well, I didn't continue after you walked in."

"I really don't care." Her hand raised to the side of her temple, rubbing her skin in a circular motion.

"Okay. I just wanted to apologize, seeing as we will work together for the next three weeks. How will you manage?" I asked, trying to lighten the mood.

"Manage what exactly?"

"Up close with me. Taking my photo from every angle. Knowing all the interesting parts of my face."

She stuck two fingers in her mouth like she wanted to vomit." Get over yourself."

"I think you're the only person I know who has single-handedly insulted me more times in the last twenty-four hours than anyone I've ever met."

She twisted her lips and let out a reluctant sigh. "Look, I don't mean to. My boss actually thinks I have a bit of a reputation for being a hardass."

"Really?" I smirked. "Don't apologize. It's refreshing."

"Well, that's the first time I've heard that." Her green eyes caught the light, and my breath hitched in my throat.

Probably not a good idea to fuck the help, Kit.

"Anyway, I need this job, so let me know if I inadvertently step over the line."

"I think I did that last night. So let's call it even." I dug my heels into the stone footpath, wondering why she desperately needed this job.

We stopped at the studio door, and I extended my hand to her. She took it. Her eyes wandered up my forearm, stopping when she reached my favorite tattoo.

"I got that one last year."

"What is it?" She circled it with her finger, her cool skin tingling on my warm arm.

"It's infinity times two."

"It's beautiful."

"It is," I said in a low voice, causing her gaze to meet mine.

4

———

JASMINE

"**A**re you fucking serious?!" Lily slammed down her porcelain bowl, not caring how much noise it made in Seaview's newest teppanyaki restaurant. Luckily, I was seated at the edge of the table with Amber wedged between us. On the other side, Lily's friends from pottery class sat. Consumed by the Benihana-style chef throwing and dicing midair, I doubted they heard our conversation.

Since my encounter with Kit yesterday, I'd come home and filled Amber in on my latest photography assignment. Stuck to the hip of Kit Jones and his band, Four Fingers, for the next three weeks was apparently everyone's dream job. But the opportunity to pick my next assignments after this gig fueled my motivation. He was nothing more than eye candy. *Delicious eye candy.*

I hadn't had the chance to tell Lily, nor did I deem it necessary to tell her before her birthday dinner tonight.

"So you're telling me, Kit, the megastar who basically propositioned you to sleep with him at the karaoke bar is now your subject? And for the next three weeks? Her blue eyes widened by the second. She reminded me of a young Goldie Hawn, petite with huge blue eyes and blonde bangs.

I swallowed the hibachi steak before I spoke. Damn, it was good. "Yes, and would you keep your voice down! Not just Kit, but also his other bandmates, Jamie, Ryan, and Angus."

"Well, fire me up with a blowtorch. Do you need an assistant?" She giggled.

"Yes, because digital media marketing makes you an expert on photography angles?"

She threaded her fingers through her tousled blonde hair.

"Don't forget, I'm a qualified Pilates instructor too! Maybe they need to improve their postural alignment and flexibility while in town?"

I laughed, then noticed Amber studying me. "Why are you staring, Amber?"

"I'm just wondering why you're playing it so cool?" Amber had that interrogative look about her. No wonder she chose law as her profession.

I shrugged. "Kit is just a guy. He seems pretty normal too, from the quick chat we've had."

"Really? How about all the womanizing headlines… the love rat, the cheat, the playboy of Manhattan," Amber added.

"What he does is up to him. I'm not dating the guy."

She raised her eyebrow. "Who said anything about dating?"

Yeah, good point.

"How does he photograph?" Lily asked, thankfully steering away from Amber's comment.

I recalled the shot I took of him after lunch yesterday in action with the band, seated on a stool, notepad in hand, and chewing on the butt of a pencil. His head was tilted over the notebook, with overhanging rich chestnut hair in his eyes and an angular jaw with a hint of stubble. Yeah, there was no issue there—he was the perfect subject in his cut-off tank top and his left arm snaked with tattoos. Even in his holed-out jeans and leather bracelets on his tattooed wrist, he was every bit the rock star.

"Fine." I fiddled with my rice, ignoring the weight of her stare.

"Fine, huh?"

"Yep." I swallowed.

"I see. So it wouldn't bother you that he and his three bandmates have just sat at the table in the corner over there?"

I whipped my head around. *Oh, for fuck's sake.*

I followed her line of sight. *Shit.* There he was.

And as instantly as I saw him, he lifted his head to mine. He gave me a slow sexy smile that smacked me right between the legs. *Bet he did that to every hot-blooded woman who crossed his path.* He didn't get that reputation by doing nothing. I straightened, then nodded back.

Some girls at the birthday party now noticed them too. *Don't squeal. Don't squeal. Oh, come on, just be cool.*

But it was too late. Two of Lil's friends had already jumped up, made a teenage shrill, and were heading toward their table.

"Lily, stop them! It's so embarrassing."

"What can I do? They're already over there." She held her hands up in defeat.

"They're probably just wanting a quiet meal," I said, suddenly feeling sorry for Kit. I glanced over, and Kit and the band were signing napkins and whatever else people could find for autographs.

I looked around the restaurant, waiting to see their

burly security spring into action. Like they had at the karaoke bar, but I couldn't find him.

"Are you going to say hi?" Amber asked with a curious expression.

"No, looks like he's got enough women around him already."

"Jealous, are we?" Lily asked. A hint of teasing laced her words.

It sounded that way.

"Fuck off," I blew out, pushing my plate to the side.

"Do I need to spell it out for you? He is Kit-frigging-Jones. Sexy as hell, fit, tanned, muscular, and tall. And you know, you *are* single," Amber added.

"I'm single because I found my ex screwing his secretary on Christmas Eve when he told me he'd be working late. Splayed on his desk, might I add."

"Exactly. There is no better revenge than shacking up with *the* Kit Jones."

"Don't you get it? My problem is I go for the wrong men. The cheaters, players, womanizers, and Kit Jones is all of those things combined."

"That *is* true. You pick men as well as I pick Powerball numbers, but you're not here to marry the guy," Lily agreed, widening her blue eyes. I swiped a hand over my face, feeling my jaw tense at her comment.

"I'm here to work. That's it," I snapped back, hoping Amber and Lily would just drop it.

"Boring," Lil countered.

"Maybe I need to be boring for a change. It sure as hell worked out for my sister, Grace. So maybe it could work out for me."

"Your ex was boring. Not because he was a lawyer but because he loved to talk about himself," Amber said, defending her career path.

"And he had a hidden appetite for hookers and cocaine." I rubbed my temple. *Why were we talking about all of this?* I struggled even to remember.

"Well, there was that too," Amber grunted in disgust.

I cast my eyes down, and when I looked up, I found Amber staring, pity in her eyes. She was there when I ran home crying after finding him with *her*. Devasted, I thought maybe he was the one. How wrong I was.

"Gone is Ajax. Kit Jones is in. I say you go for it." Amber leaned back in her chair, waiting for me to agree.

"Go for what?" Kit's smooth voice made me jerk in my seat. Standing inches away from me, his scent was a mixture of wood and laundry, and it overtook my senses.

"Nothing. Uh, hi." I barely managed to get out. My attempt at sounding professional was clouded by the high-pitched voice that flew out of my mouth.

He smiled. "Jasmine, are you following me?" he teased with a wink.

A nervous laugh left my mouth. "I was here first," I retorted.

He nodded in agreement. "Well, in that case, maybe it's me following you."

"Maybe." My lips twisted in a line, and I held his gaze. His eyes were dark chocolate, smooth, and sinful, and his lips, I swallowed the rock in my throat. It had been too long since I had a man between the sheets.

"Do you remember my friends, Amber and Lily?" I asked, snapping out of whatever Kit-like trance I was under.

"Hey, what's up?"

"Nice to see you again, Kit," Lily greeted.

I glanced around the table. The other girls were giggling and sitting upright, trying to play it cool but failing at every chance. Even the Benihana-wannabe was dropping more than he was catching.

"So, Jazzie tells me she's stuck with you for the next few weeks. How do you feel about that?"

If Kit weren't between us, I would have kicked Amber in her goddamn shins. Instead, I settled for my most direct shut-the-hell-up stare I could muster, rounding it out with raised brows and slightly pinched eyes.

"Great. She's obviously very talented. I think we'll have loads of fun. Right, Jazzie?"

I smiled. Damn, why was it difficult to find the right words when he was so close? Dressed in black denim jeans and a lightweight shirt with a healthy flash of a tanned chest, Kit was the definition of rock star designer meets uber-cool and casual.

I ignored the warmth spreading up my thighs. "Yeah, sure. Work's work," I replied, shutting him down. A frown formed across his pretty face, and I wondered what else he had in mind. "Hey, sorry about some of Lily's friends coming up to your table."

He shrugged. "It's cool. I get it all the time."

"Doesn't it annoy you?" I asked, more curious than anything.

"It did in the beginning, but you get used to it." He pulled up a nearby chair, turning it around. He straddled it and leaned his arms casually atop. Amber and Lily both stared at me, nodding.

Fuck, really? Why did everyone have to go goo-goo-gaga over him?

"Red suits you," he said, keeping his voice low as he dragged his eyes up and down my boat-neck red dress.

"It's scarlet, actually."

"Of course, it is," he agreed with a chuckle.

"What?" I could feel my cheeks turn the same shade. "I'm just correcting you on your color palette."

He smiled, his mouth wide and teeth cotton bright.

Stop looking at his mouth, Jazzie.

Suddenly, I felt the glares at the table. Confirming what I felt, I gazed around. Amber and Lily quickly stopped whispering while three of Lily's friends giggled like they were at a comedy skit.

Exasperated, I stared at Lily, but she sipped on her vodka soda and shrugged.

"Thank you for the correction, Jazzie. Can I call you Jazzie?"

"If you want." I shrugged, tucking a stray hair behind the shell of my ear.

"Well, I'll leave you to your friends. See you Monday at the studio." He stood up, and the giggles and whispers simmered down.

"See you then." I smiled, relief flooding me.

"How about a song for the birthday girl?" One of Lily's friends, Angelica, had mustered up the courage to speak up.

I wanted a huge sinkhole to pull me under and swallow me whole.

"Whose birthday is it?" he asked, looking directly at me.

"Not mine," I blurted out too quickly. "It's Lily's."

Lily beamed. "Yep, I'm every bit of my twenty-three years."

"How 'bout it, Kit?" Anjelica asked. I wanted to shove a fistful of noodles into her pipe hole.

"Not tonight. But happy birthday, Lily. I just came over to say hi to my photographer. Catch ya later." He turned to face me, his lingered gaze electric. Tingling pleasure aches flooded my body. Fuck, since when was I a horny gang groupie? I needed to get a grip. Buzzing boyfriend session, here I come.

"Bye, Kit," echoed around the table as I forced myself to look away from him.

He waved goodbye to the groupies at our table, and I exhaled, my shoulders relaxing, my body becoming less like a steel rod.

"Do you have to be such a wet rag?" Amber said, narrowing her eyes." He was so flirty with you!"

"Was he?" *He'd be like that with everyone.* "Anyway, there can't be any of that. I work with him or *for* him."

All eyes were fixed on me now. Amber had her arms folded. Lily and her friends were on cloud nine like they'd just met their absolute teen crush.

"He's obviously into you." Lily was just as puzzled as Amber.

"What? Can we just stop it? There is no way I'd ever go out with someone like Kit Jones. He's not even on my radar. No one is."

"You're on *his* radar," Amber added.

"Me and half the population."

Amber shook her head as if disappointed.

"Why don't you go for him then, Amber? You too, Lil" A weight settled on my chest at the thought of either of them with Kit, but I just needed them off my case.

"Jamie's more my type. He's dark and mysterious," Lily rounded out with a giggle.

Amber faced her. "Really? See, I'm more of your tongue-ring kinda girl, and Ryan could satisfy that need."

I looked away, grateful they were laughing and leaving me out of it.

* * *

The cake came out, and Lily acted surprised, even though she knew it was coming—she'd picked it. It was a special request that Amber and I put in with the local cake maker —her favorite red velvet chocolate cake.

The entire restaurant joined in, including the band, who stopped to sing along too. I sat quietly in the corner and pulled my thoughts inward. *Why had Amber hammered me about Kit?* Now I couldn't get the guy off my mind. He sat in the dimly lit corner of the restaurant, and now and then, I'd feel him glancing over. The weight of his stare pulled me out of a conversation more than once.

But now it was time to pay and leave. I wondered if I should say goodbye or at least say hi to Jamie, Ryan, and Angus.

I picked up my bag I'd slung over the chair and pulled the hem of my dress down. It wasn't like me to feel self-conscious, but I was.

Amber came back from the cashier, a grin the size of Ayers Rock spread into her cheeks.

"What are you so happy about?" I asked.

"Your colleague, is that what you called him? Well, he just paid for our entire dinner."

I stepped back. "Kit?"

"Uh-huh." She nodded.

"No, he didn't."

"It's done."

A mixture of feelings bubbled to the surface, but annoyance reigned supreme.

Now I had to say goodbye.

"Jazzie, where are you going?" Amber asked, reaching for my arm. I ignored her touch and kept going.

Sometimes I think Amber knew me better than I knew myself. She knew precisely where I was marching over to. I heard the click-clack of her heels close behind me.

"Hey," I said to Kit, who was devouring what looked like the left side of the menu with all the plates surrounding him. "Sorry to interrupt. Hey, guys," I acknowledged Jamie, Ryan, and Angus, who was on his phone, not even bothering to look up at me.

"Hey, yourself," Kit said, taking the napkin to his mouth.

"You didn't have to do that."

"Do what?" he asked, smiling like he wanted me to spell it out for him.

"Buy us all dinner."

"You bought them dinner?" Jamie tugged on his ear.

Kit shrugged. "It's no biggie."

"Not for you, sure, but it wasn't necessary." My posture stiffened, and my body temperature rose a little bit more.

"I think what she means is thank you." Amber sided up next to me, nudging me discreetly.

Kit looked from her to me. She nudged me again, this time not so inconspicuously.

"Thank you," I said through gritted teeth.

He adjusted his wristbands—plaited leather with some kind of gemstone—as his hazels fixed on mine. "Pleasure."

An awkward silence fell over the table.

"Hey, Jazzie, who's your friend?" Ryan stared at Amber.

"Sorry." I peeled my eyes away from Kit. "This is Amber."

She smiled at him, the flirtiest smile I'd ever seen her flash. I glanced sideways, suddenly noticing Kit's gaze hadn't left me. Overcome with a need to flee, I clutched my bag higher on my shoulder. "Well, see you Monday." I grabbed Amber's hand and pulled it, practically running away from the table.

I didn't look back and headed for the restaurant exit, only stopping when I was in the clear.

What was that?

The air was thick and heavy, very usual for February in Queensland. Yet, I'd never been short of breath before. I drew in a lungful of air, trying to alleviate the shallow breathing I'd had most of the evening.

"Oh, dear," Amber voiced and laughed, then letting go of my hand, her gaze narrowed to mine.

"What?"

"For a clever cookie, you can be as dumb as a pile of bricks sometimes."

Something bent inside of me. Maybe it was the tiredness they had provoked me all night.

"Okay, he's hot. Gorgeous, in fact. Is that what you want me to say?"

She laughed, but in true Amber style, she wasn't done. Not nearly.

But he could look as gorgeous and act as charismatic as he wanted. He was a goddamn rock star and the venom to my already broken heart.

5

KIT

I'd consumed zero alcohol since the first night I'd arrived in Seaview. The only other time I had felt this clear was after my stint in New York's finest rehab facility. Lyrics came to me in my dreams, and they didn't leave when I awoke.

We'd all had a pretty enjoyable time in the studio since the start of the week. I didn't remember when I'd actually had that much fun with the guys. It helped our drummer, Angus, who was keeping his temper checked, working with the band rather than against it, for once.

Jasmine hovered around the studio, effortlessly taking photos. More now than then, we'd steal a moment or two, just her and I. Today we even had lunch together. She seemed less like she was trying to push me away and more willing to check her feisty attitude.

Had I imagined her spread-eagle naked between my silk sheets? Yeah, fuck, I was a hot-blooded twenty-five-year-old. If I didn't think that, I'd be gay. And there was something about the firecracker that pulled me in.

"All right, let's try it again with the new lyrics." Cohen's emphysema-laced voice filled the studio.

"Sure thing, bud."

In rehab, I was taught to be grateful, and I was truly grateful for Cohen. He wasn't like others in the industry, and he wasn't fake or a fawner. He needn't name-drop to open doors. I trusted him, not only with my music but with my friendship. Something I'd had with my brother, Drew. He could never replace Drew, no one would, but Cohen and I had formed a bond since Drew's death a year ago.

Angus had returned to his drum kit after momentarily slipping out. He sniffed like he'd just done a line of coke as he tapped his drumsticks, counting us in.

"Hold up, hold up," I said, holding my hand out after a mere thirty seconds into the song.

Jamie and Ryan stopped strumming their guitars.

"Angus, you're offbeat." Irritation shot through me. I knew Angus didn't care for the band as we did.

"Chill out. We're just rehearsing."

His indifference grated like a bug that needed squashing. "Exactly. *This* is when we should get it right."

"Fuck, we're not at the Staples Center, Kit." He slammed down his sticks on the snare drum.

"Just play it again, Angus," Jamie said.

"The audience wouldn't be able to tell if I was offbeat. They just come for your face, Kit, not your vocals."

"Fuck you," I spat out.

"All right, all right, fellas," Cohen interjected, trying to squash an impending argument. "Angus, lay it out again," he boomed.

Vacantly, he pounded the drumsticks queueing us in.

* * *

"All right, that's a wrap for today," Cohen announced through the speakers, sounding pleased with the wrap-up.

"Thanks, everyone." I unplugged my guitar, then turned around to see her. I ran a hand through my hair, wondering what she was thinking when she photographed me. Did she see the Kit everyone read about, or did she see beyond the outer layer?

Gregory timed his entrance perfectly. *Did he wait outside the entire time?*

"Kit, the car is ready to take you to the radio station now."

"Shit, I completely forgot about that."

Cleaning up my image was the record label's top priority, so booking a spot in Australia's largest syndicated radio station was a start—in their eyes, anyway. The problem was, now my folks would definitely know I was in town if the tabloids hadn't flashed it about already. I made a rule to steer away from reading the tabloids. What was the point when ninety-nine percent of their stories were click-bait lies?

I can't put off calling them anymore. My parents deserve better.

"Too bad, man," Jamie laughed.

"Yeah, I'm going for a swim. Enjoy another mindless interview." Ryan smirked before emptying a bottle of Evian and crushing it in his fist.

"Fuck off, the lot of you," I retorted, flipping them the bird. Suddenly, I realized Jasmine could hear every word from her spot in the control room.

I turned around, only to find her a few feet away from me, camera packed and ready to roll. "Sorry." I scratched my brow. "That was obviously not intended for your ears."

"I'm a big girl, Kit. I've heard a lot worse. Just forget I'm here." Her full lips formed a slight line, and my eyes held onto her mouth.

I stepped closer to her, my mouth an inch away from her ear. "That's difficult." I breathe the words out in a low voice so only she can hear me.

She tilted her head and sucked in her bottom lip, making me want to rake my teeth along it and trace kisses down her neck to her navel, then between her legs. *Fuck! Stop flirting with her.*

Something told me Jasmine was someone you didn't get involved with for the night. Be it her sass, commitment to her job, or the *fuck off* she had tattooed on her forehead.

"Let's grab a drink later," Jamie said, interrupting the swirling air between us. "A soda, I mean," he corrected himself.

Why was everyone walking on goddamn nuts and bolts around me? Jesus! I wasn't an alcoholic.

I closed the grand piano, loving every note of inspiration that came today on the ebony and ivory keys. "Sure. I don't know how long this thing will last, though."

"Cool, man."

"Remind me why you're the only band member going again?" Angus asked.

"Because he's the one who's given us the bad reputation," Jamie kindly offered.

"PR calls it damage control. I call it bullshit," I snapped, picking up the nearby water bottle and clenching it between my fingers. "And I'm definitely not the only one causing trouble." I glared at Angus and the hint of white powder on the edge of his nostril.

"Yeah, if anything, it's elevated us even more. Did you know we hit number one in Uzbekistan?" Angus inquired.

"Where the fuck is that?" Ryan asked, slinging his guitar on his back. I swear he slept with his Les Paul. Ever since school, it went with him everywhere.

"Still, I think all of us should be there." There was no hiding Angus' resentment.

"When do we ever get time off?" Jamie stood his guitar back on the rack alongside his other two.

"I guess you're right. Who's up for hitting a bar then?" Angus asked.

Ryan and Jamie looked at each other. Presumably, they were thinking the same as me.

"Nah, man," Ryan said. "I'm going to go back and practice in my room."

"And I'm swimming, then calling up… what was her name from the other night?"

My gaze hovered over Jazzie, who was fumbling with her backpack. "Jamie, I didn't know which way was up the night we flew in, let alone some girl's name."

Her lips curled up, and I wondered how she tasted.

"If you're referring to the blonde girl on your lap, Jamie, her name is Kiera. Kiera Lee," she stated, not bothering to look up.

"That's it. Kiera," Jamie said. "Do you know her?"

"No, not really. She went to my school, a few grades below me, though."

Panic crossed Jamie's face. "Oh shit, tell me she's legal, Jazzie."

Jazzie's laugh was carefree and natural like the blowball of a dandelion drifting on a windy day and finding me, hitting me square in the chest.

"Well, I'm twenty-three, so she'd be only two or three years below me. So you're safe, Jamie."

He flashed Jazzie a smile—the one he gives women when he wants to get laid.

My vein popped and twitched in my neck as I watched him leave with Angus and Ryan following.

Gregory stuck his head in. "Sorry, Kit, we should leave if we want to make the interview."

"Right. Come on, Jazzie," I said, thinking this might be bearable if she was with me.

She popped her head up, her red-copper hair falling around her face down to her hips. "Sorry?"

"You're coming with me to the interview."

"But why?" she asked, then swallowed harshly. I was immediately drawn to the lump in her throat. Her green eyes widened, waiting for a response.

"Well, because the record label thinks this is a good PR stunt, and if my photographer isn't there to capture me, then it's all for nothing."

She looked down at the ground. Her feet shuffled from side to side.

What was it with her? "Do you have a date or something?"

She shot her head up. It was only the two of us left on the studio floor. Annoying Harry and Cohen were finishing up behind the glass, but I knew they couldn't hear us.

"No. No date." She dug her teeth into her lower lip, and I saw an inkling of the woman behind the mask of steel.

"Well, then it's settled." I brushed past her.

"Okay."

"Gregory, Jasmine will accompany me to the interview."

"I guess I should also come then." Harry stood at the production booth entrance. *Cocksucker.*

"No," Jazzie and I said at the same time.

She stared at me, a dusting of red appearing on the creamy column of her neck. After a moment, her gaze flickered to the floor. Vulnerability suited her, and damn, my dick liked it too. Thickening against the seam of my pants, I turned toward the door and away from her so she wouldn't dare notice.

"I'm the one being interviewed, Harry. We don't need two journalists."

"But—" His annoying, whiny snooty voice filled the studio.

An opportunity for one on one with the feisty photographer? Give it up, Harry. Hell would freeze over before I'd allow you, your stuffy tie, and pointy loafers to accompany us.

"See you tomorrow, Harry." I shut it down quickly, effectively cutting him off.

I walked out the solid timber door with Jazzie beside me, and a jolt of energy spread across my shoulder blades. I glanced over at her, noticing her lips rising into a smile.

* * *

Her floral dress sat high on her milky white thighs. Each time the limo went over a speed bump, it slipped, revealing more thigh. She rested her hands in her lap as she stared out the tinted windows.

"Thanks for coming," I said.

She turned to face me. Her loose fire curls snaked past her shoulders to her hips. Her face was naturally bare and youthful, peppered with freckles dotting her cheeks and nose. Hell, she was gorgeous and didn't even know it.

We stared at each other, an undercurrent passing between us. I like when she lets me in.

Jazzie blinked and said, "No probs. I'll be sure to let my boss know I put in the overtime." Then she turned her head away from me and out toward the street.

What was her deal? Shut down again. I wanted to know why she made a habit of shutting this down whenever she let her guard slip.

"We're here." Gregory pulled into a parking garage, presumably where the radio station was.

We ascended in the elevator in silence. I peeked over at her, but her gaze remained firmly on the floor. Then, just as she pulled her lip in her mouth, the doors pinged open.

"Kit, welcome." A heavily made-up stunning woman stood at the elevator doors, breaking up the uncomfortable vibes between Jazzie and me.

"I'm Alexis." She held out her hand, and I shook it. She held it there too long—as they all did—and I unknowingly found my gaze drifting to Jazzie to see if she'd noticed.

She did.

"This is my photographer, Jasmine," I introduced, compelled to make her feel welcome because Alexis certainly wasn't extending her the same courtesy. Jazzie's eyes rose to meet mine, and surprise flickered across her porcelain face.

She flashed Jazzie a curt smile, one she'd probably rehearsed countless times before.

Alexis walked alongside me, her six-inch heels clicking against the shiny tiled floor as she made the obligatory idle chat.

For the next five minutes, I signed autographs and chatted with the radio staff. I met the radio show producer and was briefed on what questions I'd be asked—typical questions about the band, how we shot to fame, our latest album, and tour dates. My public relations team no doubt briefed them on what they could and couldn't ask. At least they were good for something. Talking about my private life live on air was something I was not interested in.

In the corner, Jasmine sat with her camera shielding her face, focused on me. She rounded the Nikon lens, one hand on the base, the other tinkering as she adjusted the focus. I'd been the subject of enough photoshoots to know the photography basics. The brilliant photographers had a knack for focusing less on the technicalities and more on self-expression and creativity. I saw that in her. She didn't have the flashiest gear—I even spotted a hole in the back-pack she carried it around in—but there was no doubt she knew the intricate mechanics of her equipment.

I wondered what she saw. Did she just see the geneti-cally blessed features everyone else did, or did she see *me* beyond the façade? The coward with the heavy heart that only I saw? I stared at her through her lens, feeling a hint of sadness and rawness that lay buried.

She lowered the lens. Her eyes, the color of jade rocks, caught the sunlight from the nearby window as she stared back at me. Electricity swirled in the air, clamoring up the base of my spine, and suddenly all the others faded into the background, and we were the only two in the room. The air somehow became lighter because she was here. Her gaze lingered, and for a moment, I felt truly exposed and vulnerable, like she was the first person to truly see my pain.

"Kit, can you come with me, please? We're on the air in two minutes." Alexis ushered me through the glass doors just as Jazzie broke eye contact.

"Jasmine needs to be around me," I demanded, unmoving.

She stopped, staring back at Jazzie, then at me.

"Do I need a reason?" I put on my best rock star atti-tude, glaring at Alexis.

Her weight shifted from one hip to the next as she plas-tered on her polished smile. "Jasmine, can you come as well, please," she requested through gritted teeth.

I winked at Jasmine, and she quickly gathered her things, a slight smile appearing on her rosy cheeks.

"Why am I coming in exactly?" she whispered in my ear, her breath minty and warm on my shoulder.

"*No one puts baby in the corner.*"

She laughed, and the lofty sound tugged at my chest. "You've seen *Dirty Dancing*?"

"Hell yes, call me Johnny." I flashed her a wicked smile, and she threw her head back in laughter.

"Shh!" Alexis turned, and her face said it all.

Jazzie pressed her lips together to quiet the sound that escaped her mouth. "Sorry." She shrugged unconvincingly. I loved how she was anything but.

"Sixty-second countdown," the show producer said.

The radio duo, Tommy and Carlo, introduced themselves as we exchanged small talk. I swiveled in my chair, watching Jasmine handle her gear. Oblivious to the world around her and the surrounding fuss, she smiled and hummed as she adjusted her camera settings.

Who was this firecracker from a small town in the corner of nowhere?

I wouldn't rest till I knew more.

6

———

JASMINE

He's my ex all over again. No, worse than that, he is a rock star, for fuck's sake. *No one puts baby in the corner.* It was so incredibly lame. So completely corny. *Then why did the words from his mouth sound sweet, like forbidden fruit?* The kind you should never have. The type that lures you the more time you spend with it. I shook off the fluttery excitement and held up my Nikon D810. Capturing him was a breeze. With his symmetrical face, wide-set brown eyes, and a scar on his left eyebrow, everything about him screamed *seductive*. He took to the camera like butter to bread.

But moments ago, when it was just him, I saw beyond the mask he wore now. He'd truly looked at me. No filters, no band-aids, nothing to separate him and me. Not even the camera I'd held to my face.

It was the first time I'd seen that side of him. So raw. So revealing. I got the impression he kept that pain close to his heart. The pain of trusting someone only to be heart-broken time and time again. That pain resonated in me.

Whatever depths of hurt that lay within him, I felt it too. A small-town girl and a rock star unknowingly shared a common ground.

As the producer counted down the radio hosts, I watched Kit for the same glimpse he'd given me before. But it was nowhere to be seen. He'd replaced the hurt with a new mask, shutting off the pain to anyone and anything like his life depended on it.

Even though Tommy and Carlo's drive-home radio show was the biggest in Australia, their questions were still run-of-the-mill. Surely, Kit must get sick of this side of the business. I certainly wouldn't exude the same patience he had.

The producer counted down from the last advertisement. "And we're back in five, four, three, two, one…"

Tommy leaned into the microphone. "So, Kit, tell me what it was like leaving Australia to live in New York and tour in front of millions of screaming fans?"

"Well, it's pretty sweet. When you love what you do, it's not a job."

Carlo piped up, "And how about the women, hey? I bet that's a bonus."

To the normal person, Kit looked undeterred by the question, but I saw the slight tick of his jaw through the lens. But even I knew the host's question was skirting the line of what was acceptable and what wasn't.

"I guess," Kit said, glancing in my direction, and there it was again, that fire he ignited inside of me, blazing warmth throughout my body.

"But no settling down then?" Carlo pushed. The host wasn't letting up.

Kit returned his gaze to Carlo, his eyes flaring and his silence speaking a thousand words.

As though sensing his guest's resentment, Tommy pulled his golden microphone close. "Why would you, Carlo? Kit has the world at his feet, a tour coming up with a band that is number one in nearly every country. Kit, tell us about the new single."

"We're fleshing that out at the moment. But I can tell you, you won't be disappointed."

"Can you give us a teaser?" Tommy asked. "We just happen to have a guitar here, ready just for you!"

He let out a laugh. Sitting cross-legged with arms atop the armrests, he appeared calmer than a cucumber. I would be freaking the fuck out.

"Sure." He grabbed the guitar from the employee and quickly tuned it. He then crowded the microphone and opened his mouth. Rich, airy, soulful words cooed through the studio speakers, and goosebumps slid along the back of my neck.

Waiting for the clouds to clear.

Waiting for you is longer than I can bear.

It was as though he'd known the song for a decade. Yet, that line I'd recognized was fresh from today's studio session.

He rested the guitar on his knee. "That's just a little snippet."

Applause echoed through the room. "Worldwide scoop! You heard it first here on the Tommy and Carlo Show," Tommy exclaimed.

"That sounds wicked, Kit," Carlo added over the applause still going from the staff beyond the studio's glass wall.

The staff at the radio station clamored over one another, vying for a spot in front, in clear view of Kit. If I was thankful for the glass screen between the studio and workroom, Kit surely was. They worshiped the guy more than Gandhi.

I snapped a few more photos, then sat back and listened to the rest of the interview. I'd watched Kit enough over the last week to realize he was running through the motions in the interview. Polite and charismatic but nowhere near the Kit who lit up playing his guitar or playing the piano keys while singing and leading the band.

"So I guess once you've finished in Seaview, you're heading back to the States?" Carlo asked.

"We head back to New York in a couple of weeks," Kit quickly glanced in my direction, then back at the radio hosts. *I didn't just imagine that, did I?* It happened so quickly. I shook away the disappointment of not seeing Kit day after day.

"Is that when the tour begins?"

"Not exactly. We're figuring out dates now, so it won't be long."

"And will you be touring Down Under?" Carlo asked.

"Not this time. It's just the States and maybe Europe."

Groans and a few wails filtered in from the women nearby. *Get a grip, groupies.*

"Yeah, sorry, guys. Got to do what the record label says."

"Next tour, we will be back in Oz. Promise. I miss my hometown."

"There you go, girls, don't get your knickers in a knot now," Tommy taunted, letting out a chuckle.

"So I guess this is a solemn time for you then, being back in the country and leading up to the anniversary of your twin brother's death."

I nearly dropped my camera, catching it between my knees before it crashed to the floor.

I stared at Kit. He uncrossed his legs and straightened his back like a steel rod.

Was I the only one who didn't know about his twin brother? By the way Carlo asked, it sounded as though it were common knowledge.

The silence stretched out, and the studio grew uncomfortable.

Kit stared at Carlo. Carlo stared back at Kit.

I wanted to cut in, say something to help him. *Anything.* I wanted to cut the interview short. Pull the plug from his headphones and mic, so he wouldn't have to answer.

"I'm just trying to focus on the album coming out. Speaking of that…" Kit shot up from his chair, thrusting it back. It rolled a few feet back from him.

Carlo's face paled. They knew they'd more than stepped over the line.

"Thanks for joining us, Kit, and if you want to get some more of Four Fingers, check out their song now."

The producer counted down. "Okay, and we're off." A Four Fingers' song blared through the studio speakers. I stood up without packing my camera and waited for Kit's lead.

"Sorry, Kit, I didn't mean to…" Carlo didn't finish the sentence.

"Yeah, you did," Kit snapped, his voice razor-sharp. "Thanks for the interview. I hope you got what you wanted because it was your last. Let's go, Jazzie."

I walked around the table, camera in hand, as he waited for me to join him. I made it to his side, and only then did he walk out.

Girls lined up to talk to him again. The insatiable women weren't just satisfied with an autograph. They were now converging around us.

"We have to go," I said, trying to create some breathing

space between Kit and the vultures so that we could continue down the hallway to the exit.

Alexis stepped in. "They're after Kit, not you." She smirked.

"Where do you get off being so rude?" Kit glared at her.

Her face flushed the color of murder red.

"Let's go, Jazzie." His arm found its way around my waist as he ushered me toward the awaiting elevator.

I swallowed as his firm grip pressed me into his rock-hard chest, away from the barrage of women. My skin tingled as his fingers clawed at my exposed hip bone where my shirt had gathered against my ruffled skirt.

The doors pinged shut.

"Those fucking assholes," he said.

"Are you okay? Kit, I'm sorry. I should've said something."

"Can you believe them? I give them a scoop, and this is how they repay me? Fuckers, I'm going to call Marcie in PR and get them blacklisted."

"Blacklisted?"

"So I never do an interview with them again."

His hands pulled around the back of his neck and shoulders as his head hung low.

"I'm sorry, Kit."

"It's not your fault." He glanced up. His eyes strained like he was running out of air. The vulnerability took me off guard, and I purposely grazed his arm with mine.

"I should have stopped the interview," I said, guilt eating away at me.

He smiled, the weight on his shoulders lifting. "That would've been awesome. With that feisty attitude, you could have kicked them both in the balls."

"I guess." But instead of laughing, sadness tugged at

me. *Is that how Kit saw me?* All feist and attitude? If so, *why did I even care?*

"Jazzie, it's not up to you." His dark eyes lingered on mine, unearthing a dangerous need inside me.

Suddenly, the elevator doors pinged open, and I found my breath again. Gregory waited beside the idling Limo.

"I just need to get some air," Kit said to Gregory.

Air. Yes. Air is what I need.

At least with Kit gone, I might be able to do a Google search and find out about his twin brother. I rounded the car door.

"Come with me, Jasmine?" There was a vulnerability in his gaze that hit me between the feels.

"Okay," I supplied, without thinking through a response. I grabbed my camera kit.

"Leave that behind?" he asked. His almond-shaped brown eyes softened beneath the thick hoods of his brows, and he waited patiently for my response.

"Of course." I passed my camera to Gregory. "Guard this with your life."

"Of course." He smiled. "Have fun," he said, a sly grin appearing on his mouth.

I widened my eyes, hoping Kit hadn't heard him. It wasn't like that. *Was it?*

I cleared my throat and ran my hand down my floral skirt, closing the gap that caught the breeze and billowed around my thighs. When I looked up, Kit's hooded stare was on mine. I swallowed the cement in my throat, suddenly nervous.

We walked in silence for the first few minutes. The radio station was in the quiet streets of Seaview, hidden from the bustling sea frontage where cafés and bars spilled onto the promenade.

A few times, I side-glanced. His hands were tucked in

his light-washed jeans, and his tank top clung to his muscular frame highlighting his one-arm sleeve tattoos. His exposed skin was tanned and smooth like he'd spent a summer in the Mediterranean rather than a chilly winter in New York.

I'd never been interested in tattoos, but somehow, on him, they were sexy as hell.

"The foodie's markets are down here if you're hungry," I offered, cutting the silence that stretched between us.

"I'm famished." He shot me a dazzling smile, and I quickly looked away, not wanting him to think I was interested because it was obvious I saw him as a womanizer and playboy. Been there, done that. Amber seemed to think getting underneath someone was the best way to get over my ex, Ajax. Maybe so, but it sure as hell wouldn't be with Kit Jones. I mean, he was practically my boss, for fuck's sake. I let out a throaty sound.

"Jazzie?"

I turned abruptly, and curiosity bloomed in Kit's hazel eyes. "Where did you go just then?"

"I, ah…" *Dammit, think quickly.* "I was just thinking where we're heading is super crowded so it's probably not a good idea."

He looked around at the few shops on Sarbo Street adjacent to the Promenade.

"There." He pointed to a store with a carousel of hats out front.

"Does that actually work?"

"Well, it's better than nothing."

"It must be such a burden, all the women lusting after you all the time."

Where did that come from, Jazzie?

A smile peeled into his golden skin, and the intensity of his glare sent my pulse to heaven.

"It comes with the territory." He shrugged.

"I guess it's a perk, then?" *Someone gag me, seriously.*

"I think we've heard enough insights into Kit Jones for one day. How about you? Why is the fiery redhead single?"

"Oh." A nervous laugh escaped my lips. "There's nothing especially interesting about me."

"I think that's a fallacy." He shot up his eyebrow before lifting a navy cap off the stand. Stepping aside, he gestured for me to enter first. *Kit—the gentleman. I hadn't seen that coming.*

I walked inside the tiny shop and nestled my way into a tight corner to look closer at a touristy thimble collection.

"How's that?" he asked, and I jolted at his closeness, tripping over my feet as I spun at the sound.

Suddenly, his hand circled my waist, his thumb pressed against my hip bone, gripping me tightly and holding me upright.

"Sorry, I didn't mean to scare you." I took my eyes off his open-neck shirt, the scattering of dark hairs on his chest and breathing in his manly scent. With a tip of his chin, he leveled me with his burning stare, and desire pooled in my panties. *Holy fuck.*

His fingers clenched around my waist, not letting go.

I cleared my throat and leaned back. "You startled me, that's all." I rolled my lips in, trying to find my professionalism once again.

"Damn, you smell good, red."

I blinked. *You need this job, Jazzie. Stay cool.* Inadvertently, my gaze drifted to his lips. *Look up! Look up!*

"I bet you have all the lines."

He twisted his lips together and pulled away from me. I wasn't relieved as much as I thought I'd be at the space between us.

With his free hand, he pulled the hat over his eyes.

The navy cap molded to his head and shadowed his face. His dark hair spilled out, brushing the nape of his neck.

"Not bad, actually." I tugged the brim of the cap, touching his hand. Tremors of electricity threaded into my fingers and down my body. *Goddamn, was it hot in here?*

"You know, it's very quiet in here. I bet we could get up to all kinds of mischief," Kit said suggestively as his thumb brushed my lower back, and my breath hitched in my throat.

What was happening here, and why was my arousal off the charts?

Realizing I was only inches away from his molten gaze, I dropped my hand from the hat and sucked in a level breath. "You would too, wouldn't you?"

He widened his eyes." With you, red, absolutely."

"Well, I'm no groupie, Kit." I took a sidestep past him, purposely shoving him in the chest.

"And stop calling me red. I don't like it."

He reached for my arm, and I turned to find a shit-eating grin on his movie-star face. "I think you do."

My stomach flipped, but I didn't let him know that. "Dream on, Mr. Rock Star."

"Kit?" Kit Jones?" A woman appeared behind the counter, and Kit immediately let go of my wrist.

"That's me," he said, brushing past me, toward the shop counter.

"Oh my God! I just adore you!" A breathy excitable voice escaped her lips just as her cheeks burned bright.

He fished out a bill from his back pocket and handed it to the girl, who was already panting like a wild animal behind the counter. *Get a grip, woman. He's a human being.*

"Keep the change," he said.

"Thanks. Kit, can I get a quick photo?" she pleaded.

"Sure, only if you promise not to post it for an hour."

Good one. He was obviously used to being tracked by social media. I wondered how much harder fame was in an era where Twitter, Facebook, Instagram, and TikTok were everywhere.

"Sure. Absolutely." She squealed.

A few seconds later, he'd made her the happiest girl in Australia because he was genuinely kindhearted. I'd have told her to back the fuck up. Mind you, I didn't say that to Kit when he leveled me with his mocha eyes and tantric scent.

I couldn't help but smirk. Perhaps a little flirting wasn't that bad. After all, nothing would ever come of it. I was damn sure of that.

He waved goodbye to the girl who was glued to her phone, checking out the selfie she just took. Kit was in his element around people. He didn't exactly fit the stereotypical rock star. Instead, he was the team leader, band mediator, the serious-as-hell person about his craft, and dare I say it, a gentleman.

"So, what's good here?" Kit perused food truck after food truck, the smell of grease wafting from van vents and waking up my dormant stomach.

"What isn't!" I replied, suddenly salivating with hunger.

We wandered through the crowds of people, all of them seemingly oblivious to the international rock star who passed them by.

The place was jam-packed. I hadn't been here for a while as my car repair cost had made a dent in my savings, then Lily's birthday. I was seriously running low on funds.

Not only did I have the car expenses, but one of my lenses needed repairing, which had really sunk its teeth into me, clawing a fair chunk of my barely-there savings.

"Quesadillas?" Kit pointed to the truck ahead.

"I'm easy," I said, instantly regretting my choice of words.

He raised his eyebrows underneath his cap, and I could make out the cheeky grin that spread on his face.

"Damn, how I wish that were the truth."

"Kit!" I breathed out on a sigh. "Do you flirt with everyone?" I elbowed him on the arm. He grinned like a schoolboy, his brown eyes catching the dusk light and appearing green around the edges. "Not everyone," he whispered, and it took everything in me to look away first.

"Two cheese quesadillas, thanks, and two Cokes."

"Full fat tonight?" I asked, wanting to focus on something else rather than the knocking in my chest and how Kit made me feel alive again since my ex.

"And you worried about that? Please, I could throw you over my shoulder with my little pinky."

I laughed nervously. Now that would be an image. My teeth grazed my lower lip, and when I turned, he was staring.

We walked in silence, then ate our quesadillas in the corner of the park, and the cut grass served as our picnic rug. The sun lowered, splashing brilliant reds and oranges through the skyline.

The conversation flowed effortlessly, and the more we chatted, the more I realized he was just a normal guy with a serious talent for writing, singing, and playing. Everyone saw the rock star with looks to kill—*even me*. But there was so much more, it seemed. My gaze pulled to the left. *Shit*. My ex and his plaything walked hand in hand in the distance. Thank fuck they were the furthest from me, but even so, my stomach flipped into two. He was with her, not me.

"You okay?" My eyes darted back toward him.

"Yes, perfectly fine."

"So, did you and the boys go to school together?" I asked, wanting to change the subject.

"Just Jamie, Ryan, and me. Angus joined the band later."

"Ah, that makes sense. I've noticed you gel better with Jamie and Ryan."

"Well, they've been with me from the very beginning. I mean, we grew up together, went to the same public school, and when we were thirteen, we started experimenting with instruments in the back of my parents' garage." He paused, then rubbed the back of his neck, regret on his face. "Ah, shit."

"What's wrong?"

"I haven't called my folks telling them I'm back in town."

"Are you serious? They'd know for sure now."

"I'm not the best son," he admitted, staring vacantly into the crowd, and I wanted to know more.

"Why don't you just call them now?"

"What, here?"

I shrugged. "I don't mind."

He looked up at me from underneath his hat. "Ah, Jazzie, where have you been all my life?"

I blinked rapidly. My body warmed from my head to my toes in a nanosecond.

He dialed a number on his phone as though he hadn't just tried to sweep me off my feet—again.

"Hey, Mom, it's—"

A loud shrill rang down the phone. Instantly, the creases around Kit's forehead relaxed.

"Yeah, sorry I haven't called. How's Dad?"

I ate the remainder of my Mexican dinner, trying not

to eavesdrop on his conversation. *Well, trying might have been an overstretch.*

"I hope to pop in, but I don't know… yeah, I know, but the single is keeping me busy… ditto." He hung up the phone, then turned to me, lighter than before.

"That actually feels better. Thanks, Jazzie. I'm not sure I would've done it if you weren't here."

"No problem," I said, tucking my hair behind my ear.

"Why are you single?"

I nearly knocked over my Coke.

"Since when are we talking about me?"

"Since now. I want to know more about you."

I swallowed, not entirely sure how to answer. "I've had boyfriends, you know."

"I don't doubt that." He paused. "You don't have to tell me if you don't want to." His eyes etched with concern. The same rawness and vulnerability were back.

"I'm single because my boyfriend cheated on me." *And the one before him too.* I held my breath, unsure why I'd just told him that.

"What a dick," he said reassuringly.

"I caught him too."

"Fuck. No."

"He'd said he was working late on Christmas Eve, and I thought it would be a sweet gesture to bring him dinner at the office. He was a lawyer…"

"That is sweet."

Our gaze connected, and that tingle of electricity swirled in my stomach. I cleared my throat, trying to push it away. "I found him pounding into his secretary over his desk." Rehashing it still stung nearly three months later, and the fact that he was here now made my stomach churn.

He popped a thick dark brown eyebrow. "Whoever says

pounding these days?" he asked, and I laughed—any despair vanishing rolling off my shoulders.

My hand smoothed down the length of my hair to the tips, where I toyed with the ends. "Me, obviously."

"What a fucker."

"Yep." The silence fell upon us both again as I tried ignoring the weight of his stare.

"Well, he fucked up, didn't he?"

"Ajax probably doesn't think so. He and Athena are still tight. I actually just spotted them here."

"Ajax and Athena? With names like that, they deserve to be together. Is that why you went weird before when I saw you staring into the crowd?"

I tilted my head to the side. "Back up. Names like that? Your name is Kit! Anyway, guys are the same. They just think with their dicks." All professionalism went out the door after that statement. Although, in all seriousness, we were past that point anyway.

"Maybe some of us are incapable of monogamy," Kit said evenly.

Flushes of anger heated the base of my neck. "Seriously? That's the best you can come up with?"

"I'm not defending your ex. I mean, the guy should have broken it off with you instead of cheating. Cheating is the lowest act out there."

"Why can't men settle down? What is it these days? Is it the variety?" The flush on my neck hightailed it to my cheeks.

"Jazzie, take me, for example. I've never had a relationship."

What? Any higher, and my eyebrows would have disappeared into my hairline.

"It's true. I couldn't imagine myself tied down to one

woman. That's not because I'm famous or anything. Or women throw themselves at me, literally."

I stuck out my jaw. "No?"

"No. I just don't see myself waking up next to the same woman each day."

I shook my head, surprised to find a strange disappointment coming over me at his admission. "That's just sad, Kit."

"Maybe it is," he shrugged. "I'm just being honest. That's a change for me."

Annoyed at my ex and Kit for some reason, I didn't want to hear anymore. That and the wind was freezing my bits off. "I'm getting cold," I said, standing. "Let's go."

I walked with pace, the night sky darkening, like my heart, by the second.

Was there any hope for a girl like me? Did all guys want that freedom of not being tied down?

Were we all that bad? *Or was it just me?*

Suddenly, I heard my name, and I lifted my head toward the sound.

Big mistake.

Big fucking mistake.

Like a head-on collision, Ajax headed toward me. Athena, his secretary, locked eyes with me and straightened without a shadow of remorse. A smirk spread into her smug face as she rolled her hands around his. Anger bloomed in my chest, but hell would freeze over before I showed them that.

Kit had caught up, or maybe I'd slowed down. Either way, he was by my side as Ajax stopped in front of me.

"Hey, Jazzie. How's it going?" Ajax half smiled, like old acquaintances getting a beer at the bar rather than lovers, and waited for me to respond.

"Fine." I wanted the grass to grow legs and bury me.

"Hi, Jasmine." Athena smiled unashamedly, resting her perfectly red-shellacked hand on his shoulder.

I nodded, not wanting to acknowledge her name.

He had his hand on her waist, just like he used to with me. She'd replaced me quicker than a synchronized swimmer, and the anger shifted to sadness. How could he move on so quickly when all he talked about was marriage and living a life together? Heat climbed my neck and wrapped around my shoulders.

It was all lies. All fucking lies.

"Well, aren't you going to introduce me?" Sensing my discomfort, Kit wrapped his arm around my waist and waited for me to introduce him. With his cap covering his face, they obviously hadn't realized the company I was keeping.

Ajax's brazen face was confronting, but the feeling of Kit's hand resting on my hip bone took my mind off it. *Hell, was that another ache between my thighs too?*

"This is Kit." I turned to Kit, and he tilted his head, his face now visible beneath his cap. I couldn't help but turn back to see their reaction.

Athena blushed scarlet while Ajax looked as confused as a dog chasing a laser pointer.

I twisted my lips to try and prevent the smirk from spreading into my cheeks.

"*The* Kit Jones?" Athena whispered.

"I think that's me, yep. Jaz, who are your friends?"

"Meet Ajax and Athena."

"No shit!" He let out a chuckle, recovered quickly then pulled me closer. "Nice to meet you both."

Wait. Why was he being so fucking nice to them after what I had just told him about my ex?

Kit's sweeping presence towered over me. He lowered his gaze to me, his eyes smoother than chocolate.

"Jazzie, baby, shall we get going? I want you all to myself before the band comes around."

Oh damn. His voice called to my lady parts.

I swallowed, biting my lip. It only took me a second to realize what game Kit was playing. And fuck, I was all in.

"What? Wait." Athena turned from Kit to me, confused at why Kit would be interested in me.

Kit continued ignoring her, and his gaze fell from my eyes to my lips.

Oh, two could play this game.

I slid my hand into his back pocket, resting it on his rock-hard behind. His gaze darkened, and he shifted closer to me.

I smiled coyly, daring him to continue.

"You're insatiable," I whispered, just loud enough so they could hear.

He inched closer. His scent, an inviting cocktail of bergamot and tobacco, wrestled with my pheromones.

"In fact, why wait?" He tipped my chin with his calloused thumb and pulled me close.

Slowly, he leaned in, pressing his lips to mine, and I opened willingly. Sparks of heat flooded my skin as we invaded each other's space, crafting the perfect rouse in front of my ex. I knew it was just a kiss, all an act, but that didn't mean I couldn't enjoy it.

I didn't want to break from Kit to see their expressions, but I imagined their mouths smacking the floor.

But then, with his lips still on mine, he leaned closer, closing any gap between us. His lips firmer, more possessive, they took to mine.

Oh, holy fuck.

Every nerve ending shot up from my toes to the top of my head. My arms found their way around his neck, absorbing every inch of him. His hand dug into my waist as his tongue tangled with mine. Suddenly, nothing outside of us mattered. There was only Kit and me and the warmth between my thighs.

After a moment, I pulled back, breathless, heart in hand, and Kit's blazing eyes staring down at me.

7

KIT

Her lips were like the hundreds before her, so why couldn't I peel away from her? And still, three days later, why did I feel completely and utterly captivated by the redhead's kiss?

She'd looked away instantly after it had happened, and we hadn't spoken of it. Why would we anyway? It was just a kiss. That's it—all for show. All in front of her fuckhead of an ex and the doll on his arm.

I brushed my fingers over my lower lip, remembering her soft pillowy lips on mine and her soft hands caressing the back of my neck. She'd tasted of cinnamon—sweet and woody—from the churros we'd eaten in the park earlier.

In the last couple of days, I found myself in the studio before everyone else and staying back after everyone had left, hoping to steal some alone time with her. It was pathetic, especially since it was so out of character for me to seek out women.

"Good job today, fellas," Cohen said, powering down the production desk—the red and green lights reflecting onto the studio glass wall blinked off. We'd steamed ahead on the single and were now in the process of laying it down.

Lyrics completed. They'd come to me so easily the last few days, and little to no reworks were needed.

"Yeah, man, we are slaying it. We'll be back in New York in no time." Angus slapped me on the back.

Over my shoulder, I caught a glimpse of Jazzie. Our eyes locked, but just as quickly as they connected, she dragged them away.

After that kiss, flying home to New York City wasn't on my radar. But I had responsibilities to the band, the label, and myself. I knew my time with Jazzie was running out by the day.

Immediately, I had the urge to make the most of it, formulating a plan in my head.

With Harry asking Cohen a bunch of annoying questions, I heeded the moment. Casually, I strolled past Cohen, pretending to review the track on the Mac. That same Mac just happened to be the closest thing to Jazzie.

She fumbled with her camera gear, taking longer than usual to pack it away. "What are you doing for dinner, red?" I kept my voice low so the others wouldn't hear.

"Dinner?" She glanced up at me through a thick layer of lashes that coated her green eyes. "Should I bring my camera?"

"No camera. Just you and me here at the cottage."

She fumbled with the lens, and it left her hands, rolling off the desk. I reached for it, catching it just before it hit the floor.

"Shit! Thank you." She took her hand to her face in relief. "You literally just saved my job. I couldn't afford another repair bill."

As she took it from my hands, her thumb brushed

mine. I held onto it for a second longer than necessary, not wanting to break the connection. Damn, what was it with the woman and how her touch spiked my adrenaline? She swallowed harshly, and I know she felt it too. I let it go and stepped back.

Maybe we weren't that different after all. The first week I moved to New York, I worked with scratched-up second-hand guitars and slept in hallways, barely able to afford new strings. Lucky for me, it was short-lived, and after three months, we signed our first multi-million-dollar deal. "No probs. So, what do you say?"

Her speckle cheeks warmed with a rose blush. "Sure."

"How's seven?"

"Perfect." Her eyes caught the light, and a faint smile tugged at the corners of her mouth. Like a stalker, I watched her as she said goodbye to Jamie and Ryan. No surprise, Angus had already split. She walked out the studio door, sending me a fleeting smile that nearly knocked the wind out of me. A bead of sweat formed on my brow, and I wiped it with the back of my hand, unaware why I'd become absolutely besotted with her.

I paced the studio back and forth, finally deciding to pick up an acoustic guitar I'd already shelved.

I fingered the guitar, playing chords that sounded light and ballad-like. Songs flowed through me like water, and my fingers automatically played as melodic chords sang from the guitar. As soon as I heard the chords, I hummed a tune like I'd known it all along.

"What's that, Kit?" I hadn't noticed Jamie was sitting next to me as I played.

I shrugged, continuing to play. The notes poured out of me one after another.

"Fire, catch me, tease me. Ignite me," I sang.

"Keep going," Cohen directed, taking a seat on the kick drum opposite.

"Illicit me, thrill me, never leave me."

Personal lyrics poured from me, revealing more than I wanted. "That's all I got." I stopped immediately.

"Where the fuck did that come from?" Ryan asked, sitting next to Jamie.

"I'm not sure." I paused for a moment before shelving the guitar.

"You're not going anywhere, Kit. I'm turning the desk back on, and we're recording what you've got." Cohen leaped up and headed behind the glass.

I nodded. *Well, they've heard it already. What's the harm in singing it again?*

Jamie picked up his guitar and replicated the chords I'd just played.

* * *

Fucking hell, that was magic. After an hour in the studio, we'd lay down a new single, all-acoustic and without our drummer. The crazy thing was it sounded perfect as it was. We hadn't needed Angus.

This song was the quickest song we'd ever recorded. Now, I understood how Sir Paul McCartney wrote the song "Yesterday" a minute after waking up.

It just came to me like a fleeting smile and a wayward glance. Inspiration flowed throughout my veins, wanting to pour out. It's a shame I couldn't bottle Jazzie and take her back to New York City.

8

JASMINE

"You're telling *me* Kit invited you to dinner, alone, at his house?" Amber sat cross-legged on my bed, wide-eyed like a kid absorbed with a bedtime story.

"Well, it's not his house, but——"

"Jesus, you know what I mean!" she practically yelled.

"Yes. Then, yes. Okay?" I threw my hands up in the air. I'd been trying to play it cool with Kit since *that* kiss. It was a well-played kiss—an act to make Ajax see red. And it was, at first. But when his arm snaked across my waist, pulling me close, and he deepened the kiss, everything changed. Since then, imagining his full lips dominating mine sent my knees to jelly and my brain to mush.

Purposely, I'd kept the kiss from Amber. She'd only push me toward his bed, and that was a car crash waiting to happen. Been there, done that. Fallen for the wrong man too many times. Not again.

Still, this week Kit had shown a side to him I never thought existed. First, he'd shut down the bitch-hole from the radio station. Then he'd kissed me in front of my ex.

80

I'd only wished I'd captured that moment on Ajax's face, no doubt a mirror to my own when I'd caught him pants down and dick deep in Athena. But I was too shocked. Too utterly entranced by Kit's earthy scent and calloused hands to care about my ex.

"I know you, Jazzie. Stop pretending you're ice cool, 'cause girl, you ain't as calm and collected as you think you are."

She did know me, and maybe I was dying on the inside just a little about the prospect of tonight.

Amber launched off my bed toward the closet. "Now, what on earth are you going to wear tonight?"

I kicked off my Vans and stood beside her, staring at my clothes.

Amber shoved me to the side.

"Hey!" I nudged her right back.

"No. No. Oh, hell no." She flicked the coat hangers one by one, and they screeched along the rusty metal rod. "Tell me you have more options in a drawer somewhere… these are pitiful!"

"That one." I stopped her, pushing past the red and white polka-dot dress.

"Really?" She held it to my body and tilted her head to the side while assessing my choice. "I think we need something more revealing. I have a ton in my room."

I rolled my eyes. "I bet you do, but I don't want to send him the wrong idea. I just want to feel comfortable. And I'm comfortable in this." I took it from her grip and let it slide off the coat hanger into my hand.

Stepping into it, then zipping it up on the side seam, I stared at my reflection in the mirror. It showed my favorite dress but concealed my pounding heart. *What the hell, Jazz?*

"I guess it works. It's a nice contrast against that

creamy skin of yours. And your legs look like fire in that… so that's at least something." Amber shrugged.

What was wrong with it? "Remind me again why you think I need my tits and ass out?"

"Because you're with a rock god who is used to getting everything when it comes to women. Did you know he's dated Victoria's Secret model, Carmela Stone?"

"He doesn't date," I said flatly.

She thrust a hand on her hip. "Really?"

"He sleeps around a lot, but he doesn't date. He told me."

"He told you. Wow. Okay. Then why has he asked you out for dinner tonight?" She let out a quick bark of laughter.

I opened my mouth to speak, but no words followed. *Why had he asked me out? Just for sex?* The thought alone made my heart sink. *We had chemistry, but was it just a booty call?*

My whole radar with men was way off. *What did I know?* "He doesn't want to sleep with me, does he?"

"Jazzie, wake the fuck up, girl!" She lifted her arm from her hip, folding her hands across her chest.

"Fuck, Amber, I don't know. You're getting me all flustered. He's a nice guy. I'm going to dinner. That's it."

"Good luck resisting that fine piece of ass." Her voice trailed off as she hightailed it out of my bedroom.

He was more than a fine piece of ass. The rest of the world saw him as eye candy, including Amber, which he most definitely was, but he seemed so much more.

"At least wear these." She stalked back into my bedroom, holding up a pair of black stilettos.

I screwed up my face. She knew I lusted over those shoes. She held up the Louboutins she'd bought when she'd completed her summer clerkship, and the partners at the law firm she worked at offered her a graduate position.

"Fine. But only because you're making me." A smirk lifted onto my lips as I plucked them from her manicured fingers.

* * *

I pressed the buzzer, and the fortress gates glided open. *Why did I feel like I was in high school again?* My car backfired as I sped up past the steel gates. *Awesome.* Gregory appeared at the circular driveway as I approached. My chest warmed, and I was certain it wasn't from the unbreathable polyester car seats in the brutal Queensland heat.

"Well, aren't you a heartbreaker, Ms. Winters?"

"Thank you, but it's not like that, Gregory." I blushed, annoyed with myself for my inability to control my own emotions.

"Kit is by the pool." He closed my car door, then winked.

"Gregory!" I said, exasperated. Since starting, Gregory and I had become firm friends. He'd sneak me warm flaky pastries fresh from the oven. And I'd help out the band, so they didn't require him all that often. It was a win-win situation.

I walked through the marbled hallway and the voided expanses while teardrop chandeliers hung and glistened in the dwindling daylight.

My heels clicked, and I wobbled slightly, realizing I'd come crashing down if I wasn't careful. And not in a dainty—please, someone catch me—kind of way. More like an all-out face- first-legs-in-the-air fall. Now I remembered why I loved my Vans. Flat shoes equaled zero pancake-face moments.

"Hey, Jazzie." Paula waved in her starched chef whites.

"Smells delicious, Paula."

She smiled. "Just you wait."

Nerves ping-ponged in my belly as I opened the arched double bay doors that led out to the pool.

It's just dinner, Jasmine. You know you could never trust someone like Kit.

"Hey there, pretty lady." Kit sat at the alfresco table overlooking the pool, a spiraled notepad and pen in his hand. Brooding musician or model, he ticked both boxes. Outstretched, he sat in stonewashed jeans and a fitted V-neck sky-blue tee that accentuated his sun-kissed triceps. Chains around his neck hung like prized possessions, and his brown eyes, clear and bright, sucked the air straight from my lungs. He raked a hand through his chestnut hair, and it swooped perfectly across his forehead.

"That's you, by the way," he said, raising his eyebrows.

Shit. Stop staring, Jazzie.

"Ah, thanks." I quickly took my seat in the iron chair.

"You don't take compliments very well, do you?" He pushed away his notepad. *Was he changing the lyrics to his EP?*

"If I'd known I was the one being interviewed, I might have passed up on dinner." I sat tall and squared my shoulders.

A pause stretched out between us as he held my gaze. "I doubt that."

I exhaled. "Do you always get what you want, Kit?"

His stare tapered toward the pool, where beyond that, the sunset turned the sky into a liquid amber.

"Not always."

I couldn't help but notice a sadness in his voice.

"Surely, everyone just bows down to *the* Kit Jones?"

His face met mine, contorting into a whimper of a smile. "Most do. But you, Jazzie Winters, you are something else," he said, his voice turning gravelly.

Hello, dark and sexy, Kit. Damn, my sex throbbed as arousal swept through me.

"Sorry to interrupt, but here we have the sashimi to start." Paula held out two square plates.

"Thank you," we said at the same time.

She smiled as she placed the rainbow plates of sashimi on the table.

"Hope you like sashimi," he said, handing me the metal chopsticks.

"I do, thanks." *Not that I can afford it.* I took the chopsticks from him. His fingers brushed against my thumb, sending sparks of adrenaline up my arm and into my chest. I lifted the perfectly sliced fish into my mouth. It melted like butter and cream. "Wow, I've not tasted it like this before."

Unlike me, Kit effortlessly managed his chopsticks and balanced three pieces at once. "Yeah, kingfish is where it's at."

"So, I wanted to thank you for what you did the other day," I offered, keeping it casual.

"What's that?"

"You know, pretending we were together in front of Ajax."

"It was nothing," he said, dismissing it like he'd just bought a round of drinks rather than devouring my lips and sending my pulse sky-high.

I bit my lip, swishing the kingfish in the zesty sauce topped with spring onions.

"What is it?" he asked.

"It wasn't nothing to me." My voice cracked around the edges, and I hoped he hadn't noticed. "I just appreciate it, that's all. It's not often I have a guy in my corner." I glanced up at him, but his face gave away nothing. Okay, whatever. Case closed. Time to stop talking about me. "So —" My attempt to change the subject suddenly got derailed.

"Hang on, you're telling me this ex of yours never had your back the whole time you were together?"

"I guess." I shrugged. "Everything was always on Ajax's terms. Where we went, what we did." I swallowed. "My photography."

"What did he say about your photography?"

"He certainly had an opinion on it. He just thought it was a waste of time. I used to love taking photos of various landscapes, be it the sea, rock walls, star constellations, and even the outback."

"That sounds like every photographer's dream, Jazzie. Why did he think it was a waste?"

"I guess because it didn't bring any money in. He was always focused on money."

"So? If I had a dollar for everyone who said to me singing would get me nowhere, I'd probably be richer than I am today." He tilted his head and laughed. "Okay, maybe that's not true. But seriously, Jazzie, is that what you love to do?" He leaned forward, his genuine interest in me—a small-town girl—felt oddly strange, yet it warmed the tips of my ears.

"I love everything about photography." I let out a wistful sigh. "But I let that side of it go."

"So photographing bands isn't your thing?"

"No." I half-laughed, half-snorted. *Crap! Tell me he didn't hear that.*

"Ah, I love the honesty. Please never change that." He reached out and rested his hand on mine, his calloused thumb grazing my knuckles.

I tried to ignore the warmth that spread to my belly. "I mean, it's my job. It's not my passion. But who knows, maybe it will open doors in the future?"

"To do what?"

"I'd love to travel the world, work for myself, and take photos of all the amazing landscapes."

"That sounds like a pretty cool dream to me. And not that impossible either."

I rolled my eyes. "Maybe not in your world, Kit."

"What's that supposed to mean?"

"There's this little thing called money. It's used to buy things, keep a roof over your head, you know… this and that."

"Is there?" He grinned.

"Afraid so."

"I could lend you some."

I laughed from the depths of my belly before noticing his unfaltering gaze. "Are you serious? You don't even know if I'm any good or not!"

"I see you behind the lens. Even though photographing me isn't where you'd like to be, I can tell you are brilliant at it. Otherwise, my record label wouldn't have paid lots of money to the newspaper for you and your journalist friend to work with us."

"You're not *too* bad to photograph." I bit my lower lip, unable to hide my smirk.

What, now I was flirting?

"Secretly, you love it." Heat swirled around us as his gaze remained glued to mine. It created a new tingly sensation between my legs, and I had to fight the urge to squirm.

"No, honestly, the number of people who thought band practice was a waste of time or performing on the street for whoever would listen when I was twelve years old was pointless. Loads of people told me countless times to give up, that the odds were against me."

"But you still did it?" I asked, admiring his perseverance.

"Yeah. Why?" Now he was asking me the question, and I knew why.

"Because you love what you do." Kit's love for singing, performing, and creating was intoxicating.

"Exactly. It's all-consuming. It gets me out of bed each morning, my heart bursting with ideas and lyrics for the next single. It's not a job for me. Well, that's a lie. There are all the record company politics and **PR** that come with releasing an album and going on tour. It's a royal pain in the ass, but as long as I can get up and write music with Jamie and Ryan, then I do it. I love it."

No Angus? The animosity between those two we could circle back to later.

Why did I ever stop taking those photos? I exhaled. I remembered back to the time when I picked up my first camera. In my last year of school, I found a passion, or it found me. But it wasn't just Ajax who belittled my little hobby. Before we dated, my parents had steered me away from photography and into something more reliable as a job prospect. Not so gently guiding me headfirst into accounting.

He leaned back and took a swig of his drink, his bracelet clinking on the side of the glass.

He was right. Somehow, if this is what I really wanted, I would find a way to step out from the shadow of small-town Seaview and my sister's success and just do it.

"You look lighter."

I got out of my head and looked up at him, his dazzling smile hitting me square in the chest. *How long had he been staring at me for?*

"I am. You're right. I have hundreds if not thousands

of photos I've taken and could sell to fund me or just work it out."

"I'm deadly serious. The offer is there if you need a loan."

"Thank you, Kit, but this is something I have to do on my own, you know?"

He nodded. "I get it. Of all people, I get it."

"You know you just start listening to the negative voices, and after a while, you start to believe them." I shrugged.

"You shouldn't have any doubts about your ability, Jazzie. Look where you are. I'm sure other photographers would kill to be in the position you are right now."

Really? My nostrils flared.

"I don't mean it like that. I'm not *that* vain. You know what I mean, though, right?"

"Yeah, I know." My gaze fell to his mouth, and I remembered his possessive lips on mine. I pressed my knees together under the table as I held my breath. Paula's footsteps came from around the corner, taking me out of my trance.

I cleared my throat. "Paula, that looks amazing."

"Well, the menu was all Mr. Jones' idea."

"Paula, how many times have I asked you to call me Kit? I'm not fucking fifty!"

I gazed at Kit, his smile young and carefree. In the distance, I noticed Paula had slipped away discreetly.

"Tell me about Angus."

He puffed out his cheeks. "Well, he's just pissing me off lately."

I let out a chuckle. "I can tell. Any reason?"

"Not only did he not want to come to Australia, but he's also been pretty high since landing here. Being late to practice and fucking anything that walks…"

I stopped eating the delicious Japanese cuisine and tilted my head to the side in silent question.

"Hey, I've been a saint since that night."

I held up my hands, "It's not my business." Yet knowing he'd remained celibate erupted tiny goose bumps on my skin.

"Yet, you sure seem interested." He lowered his gaze to my lips, and everything inside me screamed for his touch.

Get a grip, Jazzie! You will not be another number to Kit Jones or anyone else.

"We came here to be clear and focused, and he's just gone wayward. Now I know what it felt like when I did that, and the boys tried to wrangle me back in." He shook his head.

"Can you talk to him?"

"Yeah, maybe. I should just tell him to get his shit together or get out."

"Maybe more eloquently than that." I laughed. "Ah, the problems of a rock-star life."

"It's not as glam as it seems." He focused on his tumbler of soda and lime. I only realized it wasn't alcoholic when I accidentally mistook it for mine.

"Sex with complete strangers day after day?"

Why am I going there again?

"So you *do* know about me. Here I thought you lived in this small town cut off from the outside world."

"Ah-ha. I knew the name, but Amber, my roommate, filled me in on the tabloid gossip."

His face fell. "Fucking paps. You know things have only been bad for about a year."

I knotted my hands in my lap. "So it's true?"

He blinked and exhaled. "Most of it, yeah."

I don't know why I felt so let down, like a kid watching

their balloon float into the stratosphere as they watched on helplessly.

"I'm not proud of it, red."

"The sleeping around?"

"Yeah." His gaze drifted to the ground.

"Then why do you do it?" I asked flatly, unsure why I was feeling so conflicted.

"To be free and forget."

"From the demands of being famous?"

"Yes, there's that…"

He lifted his gaze to mine, then trailed off, but I didn't press.

"Are you sure you're not a journalist? You seem to wield this power over me, making me want to confide in you."

"Positive." He was right. Conversation flowed between us naturally, like we'd known each other for years.

"Come on, let's burn off dinner."

I widened my eyes.

"A walk, Jazzie. The grounds here are acres upon acres of manicured landscape, and I've yet to explore them."

"Right, a walk. Yes." I giggled, the little girl in me secretly wanting to be whisked away.

"Unless you had something else in mind, red?" His voice was like sin, and fuck, it took everything in me to reject his advances.

"No. No. A walk is fine."

Side by side, we kept step with one another past the pool. We strolled through dimly lit pathways in comfortable silence. Maybe that's what we had. A comfortable, trusting friendship—no more, no less. *Then why was I pulled to want more when I knew deep down I could never trust him?*

"Further down, there is the man-made dam. It stretches to the size of two football fields." I followed to where he was pointing. "Gregory said there are even little rowboats and stand-up paddleboards we can use if we want." A boyish grin spread onto his face.

The dam was lit up. The black mass of water twinkled as festoon lights hovered throughout the nearby willow trees lining the banks. It was like a scene out of a movie. Pretty didn't even cut it. Romantic? *Absolutely.* Even someone like me, who'd basically given up on men, weakened at the scenery.

"Come with me," he said, his hand outstretched.

Without reasoning, I took it. Kit's long fingers wrapped around mine, pressing on my palm.

"It's dark, Kit."

"It's lit up like the Fourth of July out here."

I guess the twinkling of the stars on a cloudless night did soften the area. "But I'm in heels and a dress," I protested.

"And?" He bent down so his face was by my legs, and for a moment, I didn't know what the hell he was doing. Anticipation flooded through my body like a thousand volts of electricity.

"Allow me?" He unclipped the buckle on my high heels and slipped one off, then the other.

I held my breath as his palm clasped my ankle while his other hand rested at the back of my knee.

My heart rate picked up as his chocolate brown eyes peered up at me from the ground he was kneeling on. *This is not how a rock star acts.*

"This is very difficult for me," he said, his eyes fixed on mine.

"What?" I breathed.

"Standing here. Behaving."

He stood up slowly, his hand sliding up the back of my leg. I sucked in a breath. Then, with no warning, he removed his hand when he'd reached my thigh. My thigh ached for his touch to return.

He stood close but just far enough not to be touching me. Every hair stood on end as he leaned in. This time, though, he paused, waiting.

Without thinking, I met his lips, openly parting mine and welcoming his full, firm lips. He kissed me passionately and with an intensity laced with heated desire.

His hands found my ass, and he cupped my curves, pulling me into him. I groaned. His long, thick dick nestled between my legs. *Fuck me.* I wanted him here, now, by the dam. Every fiber of my body pulled toward him. A hand filled my hair, and he tilted my head back. He took to the column of my neck, sucking it, and I let out an audible gasp.

"Kit, wait." *I'm not like this.*

"Really?" His pupils dilated, reflecting the lighting on the pontoon.

"Yes." I breathed out.

"I thought you wanted this. Me?" He looked away.

"I do, but have you ever got to know someone before jumping into bed with them?"

He reached down his jeans, adjusting himself, and damn, if it wasn't the hottest thing ever.

"No." He scratched his brow.

"That's why monogamy isn't your thing," I repeated the words he'd said to me a few days ago.

"I've only ever been honest with you, Jaz." He rubbed the back of his neck. "I've said I'm not proud of it. I just don't know any different."

He hunched his shoulders and stood in the moonlight. At that moment, I noticed him. Truly saw him. I reached out and did the strangest thing. I wrapped my arms around him and held him. My head rested on his firm chest, and I could hear his heartbeat. After a moment, I felt his hands around me as he pulled me, squeezing his arms around the middle of my back.

Jumping into bed with Kit wasn't something I questioned anymore. It was the possibility of feelings that ran deeper than just a fuck.

"Red, you smell so good."

"Shut up and just hold me."

9

KIT

"This is strange." I gripped the red cotton fabric of her dress, feeling the warmth of her skin from underneath.

Oddly, her warm breath on my chest and her arms around my waist felt more intimate than anything I'd ever had with a woman.

"Strange is good, isn't it?"

"Yes," I said, wanting to kiss her under the thousand stars that shined down on us, then spread her legs apart and hear her pant my name.

She loosened her grip around me, too sudden for my liking.

Her fire-engine hair fell around her ample breasts, and as she stood in front of me, she appeared more vulnerable than Pluto.

"Well, thanks for tonight, Kit." She knotted her hands as her gaze fell from mine to the lush lawn.

"Let me walk back with you," I said, trying to be the gentleman she needed me to be.

Silently, we walked beside one another. When we stopped next to her rust bucket of a car, I almost begged her to stay the night. "Have I got to know you enough for another kiss?"

She twisted her lips. "I don't think you actually asked me anything after that kiss."

Dammit.

"What's your favorite color?"

"Really?" She laughed. "Orange."

"Orange, who likes orange?"

"Me. It reminds me of dusk and dawn."

I scratched my stubble. "Fair enough. Favorite food?"

"Peanut butter, you can have it for breakfast, lunch, and dinner."

"Couldn't agree more, crunchy all the way."

"Definitely crunchy!" We both laughed.

"Okay, last question. Now, this is personal."

A pink blush scaled her neck, reaching the tips of her ears.

"Music or books?"

She rolled her eyes. "Easy. Books."

"No, really?" I fisted a tuft of hair, pulling it down my cheek. "Now that's a problem."

"Is it?" She batted her eyelids playfully.

"Maybe, I can let it slide. See, now, I know you a lot better than I did twenty seconds ago."

She folded her arms and grinned. "You're bad."

"Don't make a rock star beg."

She thrust her hand to her hip. "Don't pull the rock star card on me!"

I tugged at her waist, pulling her close. She lowered her arm, letting me in. This time, I'd take her earlier lead and savor the moment. Gently backing up to her car door, I leaned down, finding her burning gaze hovering from my mouth to my eyes. Fireflies danced in the humid night air, and the soothing sound of water trickled in the nearby ponds. I lowered my face to hers as I gently brushed her lips. She parted them, an invitation I desperately craved, and with a need that scared me, my mouth crashed onto hers, letting our desires color the night sky.

I didn't want it to end, but like all good things, I knew it would.

"I should go," she whispered breathlessly. She released her smooth grasp around my neck, and reluctantly, I moved aside.

"Until Monday, Jazzie." I opened her door. The damn thing nearly fell off. *Was it even roadworthy?*

I shut the door behind her, then waited as she pulled around the circular driveway.

She stuck her hand out and waved, and I waved back as her Volkswagen disappeared beyond the front gates.

Did you send her to me, brother? I gazed up at the cloudless night sky. I was in a land that was so completely and utterly foreign, and it scared the shit out of me. And Kit Jones never gets scared. Not at a new album launch or in front of a packed stadium with tens of thousands of fans. But in front of Jasmine Winters, I didn't know my Ps from my Qs.

* * *

It was well past midnight when Jamie, Ryan, and Angus returned to the house.

Writing in my lyric book since she left, I wandered out of my suite to find them. It wasn't difficult with Angus, high as a kite and louder than a space shuttle launch.

"Hey," I said, finding them in the pool table room.

Jamie was making out with a brunette pressed up against the pool table. Ryan just sunk the black ball and was cussing while his fuck buddy for the night stroked a pool cue, practicing for what likely lay ahead. And lounging near the doorway, Angus' woman draped over him like an oil spill, doing God knows what under a blanket.

"Kit, hi." She breathed out the H like she'd taken a field sobriety test. She hopped off Angus' lap and made her way over to me in a dress that was lucky to cover her ass. Angus eyed me with dagger eyes as I noticed her skyscraper legs.

Keep your pants on, dickhead. I'm not touching her.

She rubbed my arm suggestively. "Want to play with us?"

"Nah, I'm good." I moved away from her and sat in one of the armchairs, ignoring her. I'd had plenty of three ways, but it wasn't my thing. "Fellas, what are your thoughts about staying in Australia longer?"

Ryan plonked on the couch next to me. "Why?"

"Why not? It's been seven years since we've been back here. It might be neat to hang here for a little longer."

"You're not making any sense, Kit," Ryan said.

What was *I trying to say?*

Jamie had stopped sucking face and now leaned against the wall beside me. "Is this something to do with Drew?" he asked.

My twin brother probably had something to do with it, but I pushed the thought away.

"No. And don't fucking bring *him* up here." I eyed the strangers in the room. They probably wouldn't have heard anyway.

"Sorry, Kit."

I nodded, accepting his apology.

Angus hovered like a wasp. "I've got a better idea. I'll be twenty-one soon. Let's hit up Vegas."

Marcie mentioned something about his birthday just before we left. Most likely warning us against doing anything too crazy, causing her another public relations clusterfuck.

"It's next week," he added.

"I don't think it's a good idea. We're meant to be laying the record down," I added, trying to point out the obvious in hopes of deterring him.

"We are well ahead of schedule. Let's duck out for forty-eight hours. Charter a plane and fly in and out. No one will know we've gone. Plus, I wanna go home," Angus pleaded, clearly disregarding my aversion to the trip.

Ryan and Jamie exchanged glances. Jamie shrugged. "Could be fun, Kit."

"In and out. We will be back here in no time," Ryan said, appealing to my sense of work ethic.

Fuck me. How did we go from staying longer in Australia to flying back to the States?

"For the record, I'm not keen," I said, holding my palms up.

"Since when are you not keen on a party?" Angus laughed.

"Since recently. Not that I need to justify it to you."

"Well, it's not a no, and the majority has spoken, so I think it's settled."

"Fuck you, Angus."

"What the fuck is your problem, Kit?" Angus' voice shot to another octave.

I narrowed my eyes, taking in his appearance— agitated, sweaty, and enlarged pupils. He was high as a fucking kite, and I wasn't in the mood for dealing with his shit.

As I glared at Jamie and Ryan, I stood up. "I'll go, but in Vegas, he's your problem."

"Sweet, man. You know, we've been working pretty hard in the studio. You might enjoy the break." Jamie clawed at the groupie, now practically dry-humping him as she climbed on his lap. I wasn't jealous. I'd got laid more times than I could remember. And tonight, after my night with Jazzie, I was hornier than my thirteen-year-old self.

"Want to join us, Kit?" Jamie's girl said, rolling her tongue over her lips.

"No, thanks."

I picked up my notepad and pen. "Have fun, boys."

Oddly enough, after my connection with Jazzie tonight, I'd realized sex would get me off, but it wouldn't take away the loneliness. And the guilt. The guilt I had for Drew when he needed me the most.

I flopped on my bed but couldn't sleep. Checking my phone, I noticed a missed call from Mom. *Dammit.* I said I'd try to stop by. I wondered if it would be less painful if Jazzie came with me. It was after two in the morning, but this couldn't wait any longer.

I swiped my phone, unlocked it, then pulled up her name.

Me: *I'm going to Noosa tomorrow. Will you come with me? Kit.*

I stared at the phone, waiting for a reply, but there wasn't one. Why would there be? She sleeps like a normal person. She doesn't lay awake with insomnia for half the night like me and has nothing to feel guilty about.

Unlike me.

Splashes echoed down the glass-walled corridor.

They'd jumped in the goddamn pool now, and Angus was yelling something I couldn't make out. Couldn't the fuckers at least try to keep it down?

Angus was getting on my nerves more and more. He wasn't part of the original crew of Jamie and Ryan. He hadn't gone to school with us. Employed by the label, he had become reckless and cunning.

Recklessness was one thing. But cunning. When it came to our life's work, trusting the team was crucial.

My phone beeped, and I clicked on her number.

Jazzie: *I won't ask how you got my number… but okay.*

Adrenaline shot through me.

Me: *Can I get you at ten?*

My phone vibrated.

Jazzie: *Okay.*

Me: *Gregory gave me your digits. I'm sure he also knows where you live.*

Jazzie: *Okay.*

. . .

What was up with the one-word answers?

Me: *Is okay your favorite word?*

Jazzie: *Yes :-)*

One word and a smiley face. I smiled down at my phone.

Me: *Can't wait to see you, Jazzie.*

My phone vibrated.

Jazzie: *You just saw me five hours ago. Same, though.*

Another message came through before I could type a reply.

Jazzie: *I need to sleep. Otherwise, I turn into cranky pants, and you don't want that.*

I laughed. Jazzie was adorable when she was cranky.

Me: *I'm pretty sure I've seen that already.*

. . .

Jazzie: *Hey! Goodnight.*

Me: *Night, red x*

That night I slept soundly, only waking to the melodic chime of my alarm clock. The last time I'd done that was when Drew was alive.

10

JASMINE

K *it's fingers laced my long hair as his lips traced my neck down to the swell of my breast.*

Fuck! The buzzing of my phone yanked me from my lust-filled Kit dream. When I saw his text flash on my phone, I thought I was still dreaming. But when I thumbed out my reply, and he texted back with a time to pick me up, I knew I wasn't dreaming. The idea of seeing him again tomorrow sent the pitter-patter of butterflies barreling around in the pit of my stomach. Although not entirely, I pushed the thought away and hoped like hell I could fall back asleep.

I'd missed my alarm clock from the late-night texts, and in the last thirty minutes, I'd frantically washed and blow-dried my hair, which desperately needed a trim, and put on a dash of makeup. Another sweltering day lay ahead, and I had no clue why we were going to Noosa or how I should dress. All I knew was that I felt more alive around Kit than anyone else. And staying true to who I was, was a big part of that. I picked the sea-green strappy dress with a fitted bodice and flowing skirt to the knee.

Perfect. My feet still ached from the needle-thin stilettos, so sliding on my tan sandals was a no-brainer, comfort over style any day of the week.

With only a few minutes to spare until ten o'clock, I hobbled out of my bedroom, trying to wrestle my shoe strap while simultaneously reaching for my camera. Amber sat on the gray couch engrossed in the latest *Vogue*.

She lowered the magazine to her lap and arched an eyebrow. "So, how was it?"

I rolled my lips inward. "It was nice."

"Nice, huh? "Her fingers formed into a steeple as a grin split into her cheeks. "Did you sleep with him?"

"Amber!" So maybe we hadn't slept together, but that didn't stop me from imagining his tongue between my thighs, expertly taking me in long, pleasurable strokes.

"Well? I assume the answer is no, but that doesn't mean you didn't succumb to the woman-eater. Wham-bam-thank-you-ma'am is what Kit is known for."

I cleared my throat, trying to remove the image. "He's more than that, you know," I said.

"Not according to the tabloids. He's a love-'em-and-leave-'em-for-the-night love rat."

My posture went stiff as my muscles pulled tight. "Yeah, well, maybe. But he's different around me," I snapped.

She rolled her eyes. "Oh Jazzie, come on, you're falling for him."

"No, I'm not," I said. "And I'm not stupid either."

"I never said you were. I just don't want you thinking there's anything with a guy like Kit."

I shrugged. "We're just friends." *Yeah, she didn't need to know about the many kisses.*

"I don't want you getting hurt again. Because it will

happen. Men like that, well, honey, they get their pick of the bunch, and right now, that's you. But tomorrow?"

"Yeah, I got it. *Thanks,* Amber."

The buzzer cut through the clawing in the pit of my stomach.

"Who's that?"

"Probably Kit."

"What?"

I smiled.

"You're not joking?"

"Nope."

She smoothed down her hair and straightened up. "Is he with Jamie or Ryan?"

I pressed the button on the intercom. "Hello."

"Jazzie, it's me."

"Hey, come on up." I buzzed him in. "No, it's just Kit."

She side-eyed me while I searched our tiny apartment for a bag that wasn't my backpack and could fit my camera in without breaking it.

A light knuckle rap sounded at the door.

"Hey," I said, opening it.

He kissed me on the cheek and stood back.

Slowly his gaze fell down my body, then back up again. "Wow. You're a knockout, red."

As he gazed past me into the tiny flat, I took him in—tall, muscular but not in a gym-junkie way, and eyes that could hypnotize you with one glance.

"Hey, Amber, cute flat."

I probably should have felt self-conscious but didn't. This is where I lived. It wasn't huge—modest—but it had a stellar view.

"Kit." Without further pleasantries, she nodded.

He turned back to me. "I've got the chopper waiting, Jazzie. You ready to go?"

"You're going on a helicopter?" Amber asked before I could find the words. "But Jazzie gets motion sickness."

Crap. Throwing up on Kit would not be ideal.

"It's only a quick ride. Do you think you'll be okay? I can always ask Gregory to drive us." Kit looked at me, his eyes so sincere it scared me.

"I'll be fine," I replied, determined not to let it ruin whatever he had in store for us today.

"What's in Noosa?" Amber asked like she was the commander and chief of the interrogation squad.

"My parents."

I jerked my head back. *Shit!* "You want me to meet your parents?"

"Yeah. It's not like that, Jazzie." He rubbed his temples.

Amber picked her jaw off the floor.

"Yeah, of course, it's not," I agreed, screwing up my face and feeling a hell of a lot more nervous than a few seconds ago.

I turned around to face Amber. Wide-eyed, she gave me a cautionary look.

"Bye, Amber," I said, gritting my teeth.

"Ciao, ciao. Take care of her on the chopper, Kit."

I cleared my throat. *Amber, shut the hell up.*

"Bye, Amber," he echoed, pulling the door closed behind me. We then walked down the stairs and into the waiting limo.

"Hi, Gregory," I said, sliding into the back seat.

"Jazzie." He winked.

Kit slid in beside me. Dressed in shorts and a navy buttoned linen shirt, his silver neck chains rested against the short brown hairs on his chest. Momentarily, I imagined running my hands along each curve of his muscles. I pushed away the thought that heated my face.

I cleared my throat. "So, your parents?"

He turned to face me and pressed a switch on the side door. The divider between Gregory in the front and us lifted into place.

He remained silent until it was properly closed.

"Thought I should pay them a visit. I feel terrible. I should have been there when Drew died."

"Your brother?"

"Yes, my twin brother. He's been dead nearly a year."

"I'm so sorry, Kit," I said, thinking how unimaginable it would be if my sister, Grace, passed away. I really don't know how Lily coped with losing her parents all those years ago.

"Was it sudden?" I found myself asking even though, since our kiss, I'd googled everything there was to know about Kit Jones.

"We should have seen it coming. He was really down and out."

He stared out the window. The passing cars on the highway flickered by like dragonflies.

"He killed himself." His voice almost broke when he spoke.

Tears pricked in the backs of my eyes as I reached for his hand. It was warm and clammy.

"Kit, that is… I'm so terribly sorry."

I squeezed his hand, and he wrapped his fingers around mine.

"Yeah." He remained quiet, and I didn't try to fill the space with empty words for once.

"This will be the first time I've seen my parents in a long time… since relocating to New York."

"Hang on, wasn't that when you left school?"

"Yes. I haven't seen them for seven years."

My mouth fell open.

"They don't like to fly. We speak mostly every week, though."

"Seven years! Didn't you come back for the funeral?"

"No."

No? He eyed me, and I tried to hide the surprise that no doubt was plastered all over my face. He didn't elaborate, and I didn't push him.

Who wouldn't drop everything to be back for your twin brother's funeral?

"Thank you for coming with me today, Jazzie," he said, turning to me, his face etched in pain.

"You're welcome." I just wanted to take his pain away.

* * *

Houses appeared like Lego pieces and pools like blue boxes on a Pantone color chart from seven thousand feet.

"How are you feeling?" Kit's soothing voice echoed through the headphones.

"Okay, actually." I felt less nauseous than usual in the sky. Perhaps the luxury Sikorsky S-76 helicopter abated the nerves, or the fact Kit had reassured me it was one of the safest helicopters in the sky.

His hand never left my thigh the entire twenty-minute helicopter ride. The protective touch of his skin on mine gave me X-rated ideas that definitely kept my focus off throwing up. *Maybe that was it.* This was nothing like the last time I was in the air.

"What is it, red?" Kit asked.

"Huh?"

"You're smiling. What are you thinking about?"

"The last time I flew."

"And?"

"And I was with my ex and threw up all over him.

Those little sick bags were MIA, so he was the next best option."

Kit dissolved in laughter. "You wicked, wicked woman!"

"Well, considering what he did to me, I think he got off pretty scot-free."

"Were you in love with him?"

His question threw me. I blinked, unsure how to answer or what the truth was. "I thought I was, but no. I just think I wanted someone so badly that I changed for him. So that's not love, is it?"

"You're asking the wrong person."

I nodded. "True."

"But why should you have to change for someone? For me, that doesn't sound like love. Love is when someone accepts you… warts and all."

"Warts!" I elbowed him.

"Yep, warts and all!" He laughed, his boyish grin returning. "Look down there. See that place?"

I followed to where he was pointing. Rows of houses and jetties stretched into the Pacific Ocean below us.

"That one with the white roof."

The place looked enormous, even from up here. "Wow," I whispered.

I had to admit. I was pretty lucky to be in a helicopter with this man. Not the rock star but the man, Kit Jones.

My focus remained firmly on the horizon as the chopper came to land. Kit squeezed my hand and asked me to breathe deeply with him. With those two techniques, we'd hit the ground before I'd even realized. And nausea, well, that was a thing of the past, but now, I was famished. I'd realized in my rush to get ready I had skipped breakfast.

"Here you are, Mr. Jones."

The man on the tarmac handed him keys. *No. Wait. Was that his?*

"It's just a rental." He winked as I eyed up the white Lamborghini on the tarmac. "But I have quite a collection back in the States." He grinned, and a boyish charm flared in his eyes, flipping my stomach into two.

"Kit, can you drive this thing?"

"I fucking own this thing." I loved seeing him so relaxed. "Let me show you."

He opened the door for me, except it lifted instead of out. *It was like the goddamn Batmobile.*

Inside, the red leather seats were softer than cashmere, and round dials with red arrows on the dash resembled the inside of a race car instead of a luxury street car.

"You know, I don't remember the last time I drove myself somewhere," he said, revving the engine.

"Ah, that's not what I want to hear right now with all this horsepower under the hood."

He put his hand on my thigh, sending a rush of blood to my core. "Trust me?"

"You know I can't."

His eyes widened.

"I could never trust you with my heart, Kit. But I trust you won't kill me with this piece of expensive machinery."

Whoa. What did I just say? I didn't want to be another girl he slept with, but I knew I couldn't be anything more.

"Hmm." He stopped revving the engine. "I don't know how I feel about that answer."

It's not like I'd be any more to him anyway. Right?

I needed to change the subject, *stat.* "Show me your driving skills."

"I want to show you my other skills." He raked his teeth into his lower lip, and fuck, I wasn't sure how long I could resist his dirty talk.

"Kit…" I breathed out on a whisper.

He squeezed my thigh, then pressed the paddles behind the wheel, shifting the car into gear. The car jerked forward, gaining speed quicker than a cheetah with jet boosters.

"Whoa!" My head thrust back into the headrest, feeling every bit of torque.

He turned the corner out of the airstrip.

"Do you know where you are going?" I yelled over the noisy engine.

"Abso-fucking-lutely."

I laughed. He was as free as a bird—unshackled and let loose—and my chest filled with warmth.

* * *

In under ten minutes, we'd arrived at the place he'd pointed out from the chopper. The white roof glistened under the scorching midday sun.

He pressed the buzzer on the gate. "Ma, it's me."

"Christopher! He's here!" The excitement in her voice was contagious.

Kit smiled as she buzzed us in. I wondered if he'd mentioned I was joining him.

The house was more spectacular from the ground. A selection of pale oaks and walnut timbers softened gray and white angular walls. Forest-green and olive shrubs blended into the native landscape, and between the shade of two palm trees hung a tasseled hammock.

"This is gorgeous, Kit. Or should I say, Christopher?"

He laughed. "Christopher is on my birth certificate. Kit is what I got at school. So whatever you call me is perfectly fine." He smiled at me, his eyes radiating warmth, hitting me with the feels.

"I bought this house for them when we hit number one in ten countries."

"Well, of course, you did! What an extraordinary gift."

He shrugged as though it were nothing.

"Ready?" he asked, pressing a button that cuts out the roar of the engine.

I pushed aside the butterflies thrashing about in my stomach. "Ready when you are."

"Sonny!" A bare-faced woman with shoulder-length shiny brown hair ran toward Kit.

"Hey, Ma," he greeted her with a warm embrace, hugging her to his chest.

"Chris."

"Hi, Da," he said, hugging his dad, who was just an older, grayer, and rounder version of Kit. He stood above them, holding them in an embrace.

"Sorry, we're being rude." His mother pulled away and smiled in my direction.

"Sorry. Mom, Dad, this is Jasmine."

"Jasmine, this is Louisa and Mark, my folks."

Louisa, without hesitation, walked up and threw her arms around me like I was her long-lost cousin. Her embrace was like warm pie on a wintry day—welcome and homely.

"Jasmine, lovely to meet you." Mark held out his hand, and I took it.

"Nice to meet you both," I greeted, feeling my cheeks heat.

Louisa walked back around to her son. Kit watched me and smiled.

"Let me look at you, son," she said, holding both his cheeks in the palms of her hands.

"Ma, please."

"You look handsome but exhausted. Come on, let's go inside. I've made us all lunch."

She almost skipped up ahead, holding onto Kit while Mark was more instep with me.

"She's unbelievably excited he's here," he said.

"I can tell."

"Seven years is a darn long time to go without seeing your son." He wiped his brow.

I didn't want to delve into understanding what went on in this family, but if Kit wanted to divulge it, then I'd listen. I just felt the sorrow and pain around them, wounds that were not healed and probably never would be around the loss of a son and brother.

"I can't imagine. My parents would disown me if I did that to them. But then again, I live ten minutes from them in Seaview. Kit lives halfway around the world."

We walked through the front entrance, and the ocean lay before my eyes. The glass that covered the front of the house was so clear it looked as though the ocean waves were rolling into the front room.

"This is so beautiful, Mark," I said in awe of the place.

"Kit knows his real estate. He bought this for us years ago. So over the top and unnecessary, but that's our Kit. Always showering us with gifts like it's Christmas every day. I think he does it secretly because he wasn't here…" His voice trailed off, and immediately I knew where he was going.

Here, when Drew died.

"What can I get you, Jasmine? Champagne, soda? Dammit, sorry, Chris." Louisa pinched her lips together.

"Ma, I'm sober. Relax."

"A soda is perfect. Thanks, Louisa."

Kit looked at me and smiled.

"We don't need any temptations around here, son.

Speaking of temptations, how do you two know each other?"

Oh God. A warmth spread across my cheeks to the tips of my ears.

"Ma! I'm twenty-five, and you still can embarrass me."

"Well, she's a natural beauty. What's wrong with admitting that?"

My skin was now alight. "I'm a photographer for the *Brisbane Times*. When Four Fingers came into Seaview, they tasked me to be their photographer for three weeks."

"Oh, so you and my boy are stuck at the hip then?" Mark let out a laugh.

"Pretty much. I know people keep telling me how lucky I am, but I tell you, I'd much rather my gig before this one, photographing the elderly."

Both her parents chuckled, and Kit grinned.

"I like her," Louisa said, handing me a tall glass of soda with lemon.

"Let's go out on the deck," Kit suggested.

"Perfect, I'll just get a few things ready and see you out there," Louisa added.

Kit walked beside me. "I'm here five minutes, and they're already embarrassing me," he whispered.

"Who knew Mommy Dearest embarrassed Mr. Kit Jones." I jabbed him in the ribs.

"Heya, I'm a sensitive type. You just don't know it yet."

I'm beginning to, Kit. You're not the man I thought you were, and it scares me.

* * *

Kit's mom went over and above. I imagined she'd raised him like that, caring and nurturing. It gave me an inkling into why he seemed so grounded.

"Louisa, I don't think I've ever eaten so much in my life!" I said, holding my hair back as a gust of wind blew it across my face. "That was delicious, thank you."

"You're welcome, sweetheart!"

"How long have you been in Seaview, Jasmine?"

"I grew up there."

"And is it just you? Any siblings?"

"I have an older sister, Grace. Recently, she made partner at her accounting firm."

"You didn't tell me that," Kit interjected.

"Oh well…" I trailed off. *Was he interested in my family?*

"I'm guessing your parents want you to follow in her footsteps?"

"You guessed correctly." I stared vacantly toward the sea.

"Jazzie is an amazing photographer, Ma. She's only sticking around at the newspaper until she can afford to skip out and travel the world, photographing landscapes."

"Oh, that sounds like a remarkable job," Mark said.

"I'd put my hand up for that!" Louisa added.

"Except you need your glasses to even take a photo with an iPhone." Kit laughed.

"Hey, leave your momma alone!" Mark slapped his son between the shoulders.

"Just joking, Ma." He threw her a wink.

"I'd love to see your work, Jasmine. We still haven't filled a wall in the living room."

"Sure." A swell of excitement colored my veins at the prospect of sharing my unseen work. Not even my parents were interested, yet here I was with the loveliest, most encouraging, positive people I'd ever come across.

Kit widened his eyes and smiled at me. His brown eyes shared my enthusiasm.

"Here, let me show you where I'm thinking." Louisa rose from her seat and motioned for me to follow her.

My gaze fell to Kit's. He trailed my body, eventually returning his hooded gaze to mine. My face flared as desire swirled between my legs.

"I'm only borrowing her for a minute or two, son." *Shit, tell me she didn't see that.* I gave a nervous smile to Louisa before following her back inside.

"Here." She pointed to a blank space above the fireplace. "I've tried a few artworks, but maybe a photograph is what I need here."

The space was enormous, which wasn't a problem. I thought of a few photos that could potentially suit the space. The waterfall and boulders in Crystal Creek would work, or the mammoth shot of the Bull Kauri tree I'd captured in the Daintree would set off the area and tie in with the green accents in the homeware nearby.

"I think I might have a few you may like, Louisa. I'll email you some digital copies to have a look at."

She stood, pausing like she was contemplating what to say next. "Thank you for coming today. I haven't seen my son in seven years, and he looks happy. I'm wondering if that's because of you?" Her voice softened, and I felt the weight she was carrying.

I cleared my throat.

"I don't mean to put you on the spot, Jasmine. It's just that as a family, we've had it pretty tough."

"No, it's okay. I can't fathom what you've all been through. I'm so sorry, Louisa."

"You know, I just worry for Chris." A tear escaped the corner of her eye. "He blames himself for Drew, and it's not his fault. Maybe you can convince him of that." She sat down on the couch, and I sat beside her.

"Why didn't he come back for the funeral?" I asked.

"He just couldn't bear to say goodbye. Chris thought he should have protected Drew from his demons. He took on that responsibility, and it wasn't his. And when he died, Chris couldn't bear to accept it. I think the guilt is silently killing my other son."

"Oh." I rested my hand on her shoulder. "He blames himself?"

"Yes." She breathed in deeply. "Sorry, Jasmine. I think seeing him after all this time has muddled all my emotions."

"Please don't apologize." *It all makes sense.*

"But seeing him today, he's still the boy I birthed. Not the rock star in the tabloids. He's happy, but he's carrying the weight of the world on his shoulders."

Wanting to provide comfort, I placed my hand on hers and gave her a reassuring squeeze.

There was so much more that lay underneath the gorgeous exterior of Kit Jones. I'd be lying if I said I wasn't interested in discovering more about the man who made my body surge with desire.

11

KIT

"Hey, what are you two lovelies talking about?" I walked inside. Ma and Jazzie glanced at one another as if they'd just exchanged secrets. *And was Ma teary?*

"Nothing, sweet. Just girly chit-chat."

A torrent of wind lashed, followed by the sound of glass shattering on the balcony.

"Oh, here it comes." Ma's line of sight darted around to the crashing sound. Then she shot up and ran toward the balcony with Jazzie on her heels.

"Here, what comes?" I followed them both.

"The storm, son!" Ma yelled over the howling wind.

The palm trees swayed viciously as lightning flashed throughout the sky. Furious winds, an inked sky, and hellish humidity had replaced the midafternoon sun. A tropical storm had crept in from nowhere, just like I'd remembered when we were kids.

Jazzie helped collect the glassware and plates off the table with Ma while Dad and I lowered the umbrellas and packed away the barbeque.

"I forgot how bad it got up here," I yelled toward Dad. The wind was so loud, it could contest with one of my concerts.

"It's not so bad, but every so often, we get a good one." His eyes set across the ocean. "Like now, by the looks of it."

"You could have warned me."

"Your Ma did," he bellowed, frantically trying to secure everything from blowing off the balcony.

"Did she?" Quickly, I rushed to his side.

"Too busy to remember, son?"

Yeah.

"Grab that, would you?" He handed me the utensils while he wrestled with lowering the patio awning.

I watched him struggle with the awning. More wrinkles creased his forehead and the corners of his eyes, and his hair was more salt than pepper these days, thinning on top. His belly rounded over his belt, and I realized I wasn't the only one not taking care of myself this last year.

Because there was no mistaking the pain in his eyes too.

Guilt chewed me up, settling on my chest like a bag of bricks. Drew was their world, and I should have been there for my parents. I should have fucked off my obligations and my own self-pity and flown home.

Jumping into bed with Jazzie wasn't something I questioned anymore. It was the possibility of feelings that ran deeper than just a fuck. "Dad, here," I set everything down to help him. By the time he wrangled the hanger to wind it in, it would be floating above the sea.

I gave it a yank, and the winch started to turn.

"You were always handy, Christopher. Both you and your brother were."

Drew. Sadness slashed at me like the wind.

"You know, this Friday, it will be one year since he's been gone."

"Of course, I know." *Not a day goes by I don't think of him.*

"Can I count on you to be here with your Ma and me? We're having a memorial."

"I don't know." The words escaped my mouth, barely audible.

"Son, please." His voice broke, and fuck, it nearly killed me. The wind pounded, and the sky divided with lighting. My heart blackened as the pain leveled me. It's virile, worse than the day Drew died.

"I can't, Dad! I just—" I let go of the winch and leaped across the balcony, taking the steps before he or I could say anything else. Facing the ocean, I sprinted, hurdling over tiered garden beds and retaining stone walls.

"Son, wait…" His voice boomed over the balcony, echoing in the cyclonic winds.

The rain started hammering hard, and water droplets fell across my forehead and down my face. Taking the stone steps two at a time, I descended to the bottom of the house, where the grass met the sandy ocean frontage. The rain fell hard on my face, and I welcomed it.

Hadn't I suffered long enough? Why couldn't I just pay my respects? Remember him. Remember Drew. The brother. The best friend… the one I betrayed.

I kicked open the boatshed door and stopped. Clutching at my heaving chest, I looked around, confused at what was in front of me. It was no longer filled with tools and rods like I'd expected, but a luxury bedroom with ply-lined walls and a freestanding bath that overlooked the roaring ocean.

Jazzie's voice cut through the constant rain that pounded on the tin roof.

I pushed open the half-opened doorway. "Jazzie, I'm in here."

She navigated the tiered rocks down to the boathouse. Her green dress clung to her slim waist and glued to her long legs, saturated by the teeming rain. She was a goddess, sent to me. I was sure of it. I was also sure I couldn't restrain myself around her any longer.

I didn't want her to see me this way—this weak—but I was so tired of hiding it.

She flung her arms around me, and I craved her touch. "Kit, are you okay? Mark came inside and told your mom and me what had happened. You're not going to the memorial…"

Sincerity blossomed in her feathered green eyes, and my stomach twisted, knowing it now wasn't only my folks I was letting down, but her too. "I just can't."

She let go of me. "It's not your fault."

"What?" *Of course, it is.* "Yes, it is."

"Your mom and dad told me you sent him to the best psychologists, paid for his therapy and rent so he didn't need to work and could focus on getting better."

My heart constricted, the pressure too much to take. "None of that matters, Jazzie. I should have been there."

"But you don't know if that would have made any difference." Her voice softened. "Kit, you did what you could. You were halfway around the world on tour. No one could have predicted what Drew did, not even your parents, and they lived in the same city."

"But he was my brother, my only brother, and I let him down." I kicked the door closed as tears pricked at the back of my eyes. *What the hell?*

She held me again. This time her hands wrapped around my shoulders, not letting me go.

"I'm a fucking mess, Jazzie. What are you doing with me?"

She let me go, then placed her palm on my cheek, staring right into the depths of my soul. Heat swirled in my groin at the smoothness of her touch.

"I'm no good, Jazzie."

"That's where you're wrong, Chris. You are the kindest, most loving, loyal person I know."

She put one hand on my chest, moving it over my heart. "Inside here… is pure. Never hide from that."

I leaned my forehead down on hers, warm and wet from the rain. Jazzie stroked my cheek as I stared into her eyes. Electricity swirled between us, and fuck, I couldn't resist her anymore.

She blinked, her gaze dipping to my mouth. She leaned in, brushing my lips, and as I kissed her back, I deepened it with an intensity that scared me.

My hands slid under her thin straps, stroking the line of her shoulder, down closer to her breasts.

She moaned in my mouth as I pushed her straps down, and my breath caught at the sound.

"Zipper is at the back," she said, her words breathy.

Kissing her neck, I felt around the middle of her back, finding the zipper and sliding it down in one quick motion. Her dress dropped to the floor, and I pulled away, admiring her full breasts and dripping fire-red hair that clung to her hips.

"Fuck *me*, Jazzie."

She stood at the foot of the bed. One after another, I watched as beads of water raced down her middle to her cream lace thong. Unable to watch them trickle anymore, I traced the last drop of water with my mouth, taking it before it disappeared into her thong. She moaned again, the sound a direct beeline to thickness pushing against my seam. I trailed my mouth over her hips, then slowly lowered her thong, revealing her perfect red tuft of hair just above her nub.

"Lie down," I ordered, unable to drag my eyes away from her sex.

She did as I asked and glided back. Quickly, I flung my heavy wet shirt over my head.

"Play with yourself, Jazzie."

Fear pooled in her eyes, but a call of desire pulled stronger.

She did as I asked, sliding her hand between her folds, her molten gaze sealed to mine. *Fuck me, that was hot.* I slid my pants down, and her gaze followed to see what she'd done to me. Harder than titanium, I got on my knees, and with my tongue, I plunged into her taking her wetness in long, languid strokes. I moaned into her as I flicked back and forth between her clit and her wetness. *Fuck!* "You're so wet, baby. I want to lap you up."

She thrust her hips into me as I took her deeper. Her hands pulled at my hair.

"Kit, fuck." Her pussy clenched around my tongue, and I thrust deeper until she saw stars.

I stared at her, her lips the color of deep roses, her face flushed. I grew hungrier for her.

"We're not done yet. Roll over, knees up, red."

A grin spread onto her lips. Yes, baby, I want to show you real pleasure.

Standing on the edge of the bed, I ran my hand down the creamy contours of her back. She shuddered and rolled closer to me. Her vibrant red hair splayed to the side, and I swatted her delicious ass, then filled her with two fingers stretching her. She let out a moan, and my dick throbbed. Fuck, I couldn't wait any longer.

I removed my hand, and the sound of her wetness

filled the room. I quickly wrapped myself, and when I looked up, Jazzie's eyes were set on mine, her teeth dragging along her bottom lip.

Without warning, I sunk into her. My eyes rolled back into my head. Fuck, I've wanted her since I saw her at the bar. I opened her up with each stroke.

"Fuck, red," I breathed out.

She arched her back as I entered her deeper, hitting her G-spot, then I picked up speed, holding her hips and filling her over and over again. The ocean roared in the background, masking our moans and gasps.

Quickly, I flipped her over onto her back. I needed to see her. She tugged her hands in my hair as I took her and kissed her breathlessly. I held off, knowing she was close, but every nerve ending felt like it had been ignited by her touch.. The sound of her moans tipped me over, and I couldn't hold back any longer. With a rush of blood, my muscles tightened and clenched like a fist until suddenly, the raging waves released inside me.

"Kit," she moaned, fisting my hair and finding her release underneath me.

12

JASMINE

It took only a millisecond for his hooded gaze to pool desire in my lower belly. He needed me, and somewhere inside me, where there was space with no common sense or thinking, I knew I had to have his body on mine.

But what the fuck?

Laying on his bare chest, under its rise and fall, I listened to his steady heartbeat. We silently stared out the window where the ocean lay at the foot of the boathouse, and its waves crashed against the rocks one after another. The darkened clouds floated away, letting in the afternoon's light. *What had we done?*

"Thanks for following me down here, Jazzie." He stroked my hair in a soothing motion.

He just gave me two mind-blowing orgasms. Shouldn't I be thanking him? I exhaled. Predictably, he'd lived up to the tabloids. He knew sex like I knew how to take the perfect photo. My mind went into overdrive. I was set up to fail. I wasn't a one-time kind of girl and never had been. I'd only ever had relationships, never sex and dash. But Kit wouldn't want anything different. He tilted my chin up. "What is it?" He searched my face for the answer, pulling aside the strand of hair that fell across my cheek.

Dammit. Why did he have to look so sincere?

"It's nothing."

"I know a lot of liars in my line of work, Jazzie. Please don't be one of them."

"I've just come out of a pretty fucked-up relationship, and I'm just confused about what just happened."

There, I said it.

He raked his hand through his hair then it swooped across his forehead—the same possessive hand that left a burning mark on my skin. "Well, that makes two of us."

He caught my stare, and I traced the infinity tattoo on his arm, trying to decipher the conflicting emotions inside me.

He closed his eyes, inhaling sharply. "Why do I get the feeling you don't do this every day?"

"What?" I stopped circling his tattoo, slightly pulling back, ready to defend myself.

"No! That's not what I meant." He shook his head. "The sex was amazing, Jazzie. Intimate and... what I meant to say is, you don't just dive into casual sex, do you?"

He's even calling it casual.

"No. I've always been in a relationship."

"You know I never have."

"That's why I can never trust you, Kit."

He closed his eyes momentarily, then opened them. "I know."

I rested my head on his solid chest, fingering his snail trail of dark hairs.

"Can I trust you to just go with whatever this is?" he asked. "I will if you will?"

He tilted my chin to meet his gaze. Vulnerability laced his chocolate eyes. The sincerity was there. *I was certain of it.*

Whatever this was, I felt alive. There was no harm in just seeing where it went. *Was there?*

My muscles stiffened involuntarily before I took a deep breath to push away the fear. "Deal."

His smile was contagious.

He snaked his arm around my waist and pulled me on top of him. My breasts pressed into his chest, and my hair fell to the side of his face as we locked lips. Uncertainty and exhilaration coursed through my bones. He cupped my ass and pressed me into his firm and full erection.

I moaned into his mouth as he kissed me with more force and something else. *Something that felt like it was only for me.*

I pulled away from his kiss, gasping for air. "Kit, we shouldn't…"

"But you're too fucking delicious, red," he said, finding my wetness.

"Ah," I moaned. "Chris."

He stopped playing me like a guitar and stared at me.

"What? I like it better than *Kit.*"

"Do you now?" He smirked. "You know what I like, red?" His fingers traced my upper thigh, climbing higher and higher.

Wetness started to pool between my thighs as the ache for him grew stronger. Without thinking, I rolled off him. It was the only way I could stop myself from having mind-blowing sex with him again.

"Jazzie, you're killing me." He reached for me, but I'd already moved far enough away to remain outside his grasp.

"Your parents are probably wondering where we are."

I breathed, trying to get a grip on the desire raging inside of me.

"So?"

A smirk peeled into my burning cheeks. "We have time later."

"Promise?"

I giggled. "Promise."

"You know, you're the first girl ever to turn me down. Not once but twice now!"

"Did I bruise your precious ego?"

He laughed. "It's brutal but refreshing."

I peeled my dress off the floorboards and stepped into it.

He watched me dress, tracing my thighs to my breasts, then finally my face. My skin heated like a forgotten light bulb.

"There's a vision, red."

Damn, I liked it when he called me that now. It sounded dirty, forbidden, and made just for me.

I smiled, reminding myself I was naked around Kit Jones. Surprisingly, it felt so normal and natural.

He rolled off the bed and stood in his birthday suit. The warm rays of sunlight streamed into the double doors, kissing his olive skin. His body was a triumph of muscles, perfectly sized biceps, and gym-honed abs that led to his delicious V-cut. *Damn.* He put his hands behind his head. "Things are so much simpler here. Slower."

I zipped up my dress, finally wrangling the wet rag onto my frame. "What's New York City like? It's been at the top of my bucket list to go there."

"It's a concrete jungle, full of chaos and parties. But it's been home for the last seven years."

He grabbed his Calvin Klein boxer briefs off the floor.

"It's an amazing city, but it can also tear you down if you let it."

"How so?"

"Since losing Drew, I pushed myself into writing, recording, and working over eighty hours a week most weeks. Then I drowned myself in endless parties, endless women, and alcohol on tap. It's so easy to lose yourself." He stared vacantly toward the horizon. "Recently, it got pretty bad. I'd been out partying for two weeks straight. That's when the record company said enough is enough, and they flew us here."

"To escape the bad press?"

"Exactly. Focus on recording the new single. What they didn't realize is that I'd be here when it was Drew's one-year anniversary."

"I'd like to come to the memorial with you if you'd let me."

He turned, facing me, but said nothing. I saw the pain return in his eyes. "Your dad told me it's on Friday."

"It is."

"Let me share the pain with you, Chris."

"I don't know, Jaz."

"Just think about it?" I lifted my head, holding firm eye contact with him.

"Okay."

I picked his shirt off the floor and handed it to him. He held onto my hand, not letting go when I tried pulling away. "Maybe you are my medicine, Jazzie." He planted a soft kiss on my lips before pulling away and sliding into his shirt.

I exhaled. I knew Kit could pen lyrics, but still, his words struck a chord.

Don't get attached, Jazzie.

* * *

The last forty-eight hours were a dream. I didn't coo over celebrities, even if they were sexy-as-hell rock stars with hair softer than mine and morish chocolate eyes you could wade in.

But Kit *Christopher* Jones was something else.

He didn't fit the rock-star cliché. Being vulnerable, honest, and putting my needs above his was not at all what I'd expected. Nor was the way his hands intimately planed the surface of my skin, feeling every contour of my body. Now, I was halfway in and scared as hell because Amber said it first. She knew it before me. I was falling for him, fully aware of how it would end, but unable to help myself from plummeting into the head-on collision.

He would be gone, back to the US, and I'd be here.

He'd be splashed across billboards and tabloids, and I'd still be here.

I was residing in my shitty newspaper job, earning barely enough to get by where days stretched into long months. Kit would forget about me the instant he left Seaview, yet he'd be a permanent reminder during my daily grind.

"Jasmine, you haven't touched your food." I jolted from my impending doom.

I didn't know what was worse, the impending collision with the Mac truck or dinner with the parents and my successful sister, Grace, and Russell, her perfect fiancé.

I picked at my rump steak, wondering when this thing with Kit would kick me in the teeth and knock me out flat, just like those before him had.

"So, how's the job with Four Fingers going?" Grace asked, looking immaculate in her black pencil skirt and silk blouse. She screamed power boss and successful. All the things my parents tried carving out for me.

"Great. They're a friendly bunch of guys to work with, Kit too." *Keep it vague. Good idea.* It sounded better than *Kit is a fucking God in the sack yet more grounded than your fiancé, and somehow already etched on my heart.*

"Friendly?" She raised her eyebrows so far they stretched into her pulled-back bun. "Womanizer and playboy and reckless, I think were some words the tabloids used to describe Kit, and you use friendly?"

I continued to toy with my steak and wondered if he was feeding the press on his trip to Vegas. He'd left this morning for his drummer's birthday. He'd said he didn't want to go, that he'd wanted to stay with me, but he had to for band morale. They were flying in and out on a private jet and would be back in forty-eight hours. Forty-eight hours without his hands worshipping every inch of my body was too long to bear.

"Believe nothing you read, Gracie."

"Jasmine, we don't play with our food. We eat it." *Fuck's sake, how old was I?*

"Okay, Dad." I sighed, wishing I'd gone with Amber and Lily to sushi rather than being the fifth wheel on a wonky ride.

"Well, I have some news," Russell said, beaming from ear to ear.

"Oh, go on," Mom said, her voice higher.

Here we go. What was it this time? Maybe he rescued a litter of cats from their non-lactating mother. Or better still, he actually parted with some of his own money and gave some to charity.

"Gracie and I put a deposit on a six-bedroom house today."

Six? Why, 'cause five was too small? Right, didn't see that one coming.

The clanging of cutlery hit the table. "What? Where?" Dad asked.

Russell and Grace smiled at one another. They were so happy, and he was perfect for her.

A successful business owner, Russell owned seven franchised cafés from Byron Bay to Brisbane.

"In Seaview, of course! Down on Waterside Drive."

The best street in the suburb, why would they buy anywhere else?

Mom pushed her chair aside. Rushing over, she gave them both a bear hug.

Dad smiled proudly. "Congratulations, how wonderful, Gracie. I want to know all about it." Dad angled his seat to face her and Russ. They were all enamored in deep conversation. Words like fireplaces, water views, and luxury walk-in closets were thrown around, dragging me into a spiral of negativity about my inability to make ends meet.

My phone beeped, and I welcomed the interruption as an escape from my negativity loop.

Kit: *Just arrived. Miss you x*

A tingling warmth shot up my legs and hit my thighs, replacing the gray cloud above my head. *Kit missed me?*

"What's so important, Jasmine? Your sister is telling us all about her place." Mom glared at me, annoyed at my apparent lack of eagerness.

"Nothing. It's nothing. I'm excited for you both," I bumbled out. I wasn't lying. I *was* happy for her and Russell. *Was it just too much to want that for me?*

"Russell, have you ever considered sharing the load? I'm sure Jasmine could be useful somehow," Dad suggested.

Fuck, here we go again. "I'm right here, Dad, and in case you forgot, I have a job."

"I'm sure I could find something." Russell scratched the bridge of his nose. "Actually, there is someone who is about to take a year of maternity leave, and I'm struggling to find a suitable replacement. I'm sure we can train you and get you up to speed," Russell sipped his pinot, completely oblivious to my feelings on the topic.

"What is it that she does?" Dad asked, pressing him further.

Hello? Was I even here?

"She manages four of my cafés in the city."

Dad jutted out his chin, thinking about it. "That sounds like a solid, respectable job, Jasmine."

Fuck's sake. I'd rather go head-to-head with a lion than work for Russell in a soul-crushing job.

"Oh, honey, why don't you look at it?" Mom pleaded with her weathered green eyes.

I steepled my fingers on the table and leaned back in my chair. "Thanks. But I have a job, remember?"

"One that barely pays you, if I recall. Russ is doing you a favor here, sis. Maybe it's time you listened," Grace added, throwing me her best attempt at an authoritative big sister know-it-all stare.

Why did she have to get up in my face? Yes, you finished college, and I didn't. Yes, you completed the degree Mom and Dad saved for since we were kids, and I didn't. I'm not perfect.

"I like photography." *Well, I did before I completely lost myself in my ex.*

"Just consider it," Grace added.

I pushed away my cold steak. The warmth Kit's text showered me in had now been replaced with anger from the pathetic attempt to bully me into a job I had zero interest in.

"Sure," I said. "I'll think about it." I tossed my hair behind my ear, knowing that's what they wanted to hear and just to shut everyone up for the minute. "I'd love to stay for dessert, but I'm not feeling the best."

"Oh?" Mom inquired.

Grace narrowed her eyes. "It's probably all the hours you're putting in."

Note to self, do not confide in my sister about shitty days on the job.

Bristling in my seat, I gripped the bottom of the chair, curling my hand around it in frustration. Sitting here with a target on my back was getting old. I was the bullseye to their arrows and needed to get the hell out of the Spanish Inquisition that lay dead ahead.

"We can't all be perfect, Grace."

"Oh, why not?" My jaw clenched, and my knuckles burned as I clawed at the seat with a tiger grip.

"Because it's boring."

"Boring pays, Jazzie." Grace deadpanned.

"Just for once, Grace, be quiet," I snapped, pushing my chair out. I shot up, eager to get out.

"Girls, girls come on," Dad remarked. It wasn't often we fought, but lately, we'd turned it up a notch.

"Jasmine, dear, let me walk you out." Mom pulled out her chair. She was always the peacekeeper in the family, but sometimes I wondered if she had any thoughts of her own.

I kissed Dad on the head, noticing the large balding patch he'd tried covering up with the comb-over. *Didn't work.*

They were getting old, and they just wanted the best for me. I got it. They'd saved to put me through college. It wasn't my fault I couldn't sit there and learn numbers. I honestly couldn't imagine anything worse than sitting in a course for four years and getting a degree that was more boring than watching paint dry.

Reluctantly, I went over to hug my sister.

She clawed me in a big bear hug. "I'm here if you need me."

I nodded, pushing away the unexpected emotion welling in my chest.

13

KIT

Lyrics flowed like an avalanche, and in the fourteen hours it took from Brisbane to McCarran International Airport in Las Vegas, I'd penned lyrics to three new songs.

Between writing and imagining her alabaster long legs wrapped around my waist and copper-red hair trailing down her bare back, by the time we arrived at Club Marquee, exhaustion had riddled me, and I wasn't in the mood to party.

So much for coming in after dark and flying under the radar. I'd already signed a shit-ton of autographs, and it was nearing midnight. At least we had a private floor to ourselves that overlooked the club. Jonesy, our private security, had teamed up with a local guy. Together, they guarded the floor like *The Blues Brothers*, turning away unwanted guests and fans from entering.

"Drink up, boys!" Angus yelled over the pounding bass, downing his tumbler of whiskey.

The lights flickered and pulsed to the beat. Always wanting to one-up us, he had a girl on each knee. The blonde leaned into his chest, showing her bare ass to the rest of us. The other girl, who looked barely legal, was dressed in a bra and shorts.

I sipped on a beer. I could have one beer and drink it slowly. That way, the boys wouldn't know how many I'd had. I didn't fucking care anyway. That little asshole, Angus, was already high. I knew I was in control. The last few days, I felt more together than I had in the last year.

"Kit, baby, can I sit here?" A platinum blonde with fake tits the size of cantaloupes sat beside me.

"Sure," I said in my most platonic voice.

"This is awesome!" Ryan returned from the bar, holding a magnum of alcohol in each hand.

"Yeah, swell," I said less than enthusiastically. Hovering around me were beautiful, sexy women, but none were *her.* Jazzie wasn't here, but she remained with me. Even halfway across the globe, she'd stayed on my mind and, oddly, in my heart. She'd cushioned the blow to my black heart and was an addiction I craved.

My phone flashed, and I grabbed it quickly.

Jazzie: *Miss you too, Chris. Dinner with the family sucked.*

Damn, I liked it when she called me Chris. I reread the text wanting to be near her, ignoring the buzz of music, drunken laughter, and women and wanted to know exactly why it sucked. But I couldn't call, not here. I remembered she said her parents wanted her to go to college, but she didn't. How her sister climbed the ranks and was uber-successful in a job where numbers mattered, and according to Jazzie, she didn't.

I shot a text back.

Me: *Sorry, Jaz. We can't all be perfect.*

My phone lit up after a few seconds.

Jazzie: *Are you already making excuses?*

Fuck. That's not what I meant.

Me: *Red, it's only you on my mind. I'm referring to your sister.*

I stared at my phone, waiting for it to flash with her name. After what felt like an eternity, the screen lit up.

Jazzie: *Right, well… you know I can't trust you.*

My shoulders slumped as I thumbed out a reply.

Me: *I know.*

I tapped my foot against the marble table dotted with beers, bottles, and cocktails.

What if I could convince her she could trust me? But how? *Could I even trust myself?* Gorgeous women surrounded me, willing to do whatever I asked of them. Having whatever I desired was as easy as breathing. It had become boring. But I didn't want them. I wanted Jasmine. But would that change tomorrow? It all could change in a heartbeat, like when Drew downed a bottle of pills and ended his life. It could all come crashing down.

"Kit, you all right, bud?" Ryan slapped my knee, breaking my swirling thoughts.

"Yeah, just not feeling it."

"Sweet cheeks, give us a minute, yeah?" He kissed the girl on top of him and whispered something in her ear I didn't want to fucking know about. She got up and smiled as she headed toward the bar.

She batted her eyelashes at me, and I politely smiled. I wasn't doing anything wrong, but why did it feel like it? We hadn't set any ground rules for whatever this was between Jazzie and me, but we said it was worth exploring. So what the fuck was I doing here when time was running out?

"What's up? You've been so quiet these last few days. You and that photographer have been spending so much time together. You tapping that?"

"She's not like that, Ry." He raised his eyebrow, and I sighed into my drink. "I don't want to get into it."

"Come on, Kit. I've known you since we were kids."

I exhaled. "I'm thinking about going to Drew's memorial on Friday, and I think I want to stay in Seaview for a while."

"Wow, man, I think that's a courageous move going to the memorial. Let me know if you want me to come with you. About staying longer in Australia…" He flicked his tongue ring back and forth across his lips. "Is Jazzie the reason you want to stay longer?"

I rubbed at my temple. "Yes, she's part of it, but also, we haven't had a break since leaving school. I'm fucking tired."

He picked up his beer and sucked it back. "I hear you. But mini-breaks like these, now, we can rest, chill, and recharge."

"This is not recharging. Drinking 'til we are blind drunk, fucking around, then returning to the studio isn't my idea of a recharge."

"It's rock and roll, Kit. We just gotta keep rolling with this crazy wave. One day it could all stop."

"I know." *I knew more than anyone how quickly things could change.*

"So let's just keep it going. We have the tour when we get back. You love touring."

"I guess." *I just want more now.*

"Come on, enjoy tonight. I know you've had a beef with Angus lately, but he's cool."

"He's a cunt."

He laughed. "He can be, but let me remind you, so can you." He elbowed me in the ribcage.

"Fuck off."

"I will. Now, if you don't mind, I have a gorgeous fuck waiting for me I need to get to."

I shook my head.

"*You*, of all people, are judging *me*?" Ryan threw his

head back, laughing. "Kit Jones, she's got you by the balls. For now, anyway." He stood up and slapped me square on the shoulders.

I squinted, but it wasn't from the strobe lighting. Maybe Jazzie had taken my black-inked heart, but I didn't want to give it to another soul. Not now. But would I get tempted? She knew she couldn't trust me. Monogamy isn't natural. *Right?*

I stared at my dark phone screen as I drank my lime and soda. Knowing she'd be asleep, I swept my gaze around the club and tried to relax. Ryan drew back on his cigarette, shining with a post-cum glow. A woman twirled Jamie's black curls while they chatted for hours about fuck knows what. Then there was Angus. He'd already been through two women, disappearing with both.

Hours passed. Too many to count. I knew the jet was on standby, but as I thought the night was ending, Angus invited another group of women into the VIP area.

"This one's for you, Kit. Looks like you need a bit of help tonight," Angus said, flopping onto the lounge.

The kid had some fucking nerve. I bit my tongue and gandered at the scantily clad girl casting fuck-me eyes. "I'm okay, sweetie, thanks."

"You won't regret it, Kit." She widened her legs, her split opening high onto her thigh.

Jesus, what the fuck is wrong with me? She'd give the best models in town a run for their money, and here I was, saying no.

"I'm sure, but I'll pass."

Angus stood up, unsteady on his feet. "What the fuck, Kit?"

Here we go.

"I appreciate it, Angus, but I don't need any help getting laid."

"She's gorgeous." He pulled his arm around her waist.

She smiled at him, then focused on me, biting her lower lip.

"She is. But I'm not interested."

"Is this because of the photographer?"

Fuck, was I that obvious? "This has nothing to do with you, Angus. Just go, have your fun."

"This has everything to do with me. I'm the goddamn drummer and what you say affects all of us."

I shook my head, hoping he'd let it go.

"She's the reason you want to stay in Oz?"

He sure had an excellent memory of our chat around the pool table for a drunk who was high as a kite.

I was growing irritated with his line of questioning. "Yeah, maybe. I dunno."

"Well, you don't get to decide our fate, Kit." The pad of his finger pointed toward my face.

I inhaled deeply. Otherwise, I would have grabbed his finger and shoved it up his ass. "I'm not deciding anything."

"Good, because if your decisions are anything like your twin, they don't end well."

I leaped up, my tired body overrun with adrenaline, every muscle tensed and alight with fire. "Fuck you, Angus!" I screamed, my arm pushed forward into his face, my fist connecting with his nose. He fell backward, furniture breaking his fall on the way to the floor. Girls shrieked and ran away from the scene, and Jamie and Ryan yelled something, but I didn't care. I launched at him again. Blow after blow, I pounded his face.

"Fuck you, Kit." He spat blood out as he fisted his hands into a ball, striking back. But his punches were pansies.

Hands on my shoulders gripped me, pulling me and

my fist off his face. I fought against whoever held me back and lurched toward him again, landing another blow. Blood stained his pretty face. More hands on my body pulled me off of him. This time, I couldn't fight the pull of people holding me back.

"Fuck, Kit, you've fucked up his face," Jamie yelled over the music.

"It was fucked up to begin with," I spat out. In my peripheral, I saw Jonesy running toward us. *Fuck.*

Jamie and Ryan had their arms outstretched on my chest, forcing me back while Jonesy tended to Angus.

"Jesus. Fuck, Kit, it's the kid's birthday," Ryan's voice cut through the screams of women.

"I don't give a fuck. Did you hear what he said about Drew?"

The girls had backed away from the VIP area as more security cleared the crowd. Angus clutched his head as he lay groaning like the little punk-ass bitch he was.

"Yeah, he was being an ass, but he's drunk. We all are. He talks shit, and you let it slide."

I wriggled my arm free from their hold and wiped away the bead of sweat that had formed on my brow with the back of my hand. "Not anymore."

* * *

Jamie hung up. "Jesus, fuck." He'd spent the last twenty minutes groveling to Marcie, head of public relations for the band.

"Not good?" Ryan shot up an eyebrow.

"What the fuck do you think?" He lifted his scowl briefly, then reverted down to his phone.

Our two-day bender in Vegas had turned out to be a nightmare of epic proportions. Somehow, someone snuck a camera into the VIP room and snapped a few photos. And they got the money shot—the one where my fist flew off Angus' face. Now, we were in the same shit soup we'd been trying to escape since leaving New York.

Jamie stared at his phone.

"*Kit Drums into the Drummer's Nose.* Marcie liked that one the best. Splashed across the front page of the *Vegas Daily* too, just in case anyone missed it. Or, *Kit Jones on a Path of Destruction. Variety Magazine* had a full-page article devoted to that tidbit of information."

"They're just trying to get clicks." I shrugged, staring at the wayward palm trees that lined the Seaview Beach promenade. I'd never been so happy to see Gregory and the car that waited for us on the tarmac. Thanks to him, I was one step closer to seeing *her.*

"Did you see this one?" Jamie shoved his iPhone in my face. My fist, bloodied and clenched, wielded to throw another punch while Jamie and Ryan attempted to pull me back. I smiled. Well, I never said it was my finest moment.

"It's not a fucking joke," Jamie snapped. "Marcie is so mad. I can't even begin to tell you—"

"I heard her." It was hard not to. Her high-pitched voice shouted down the line and over Jamie's attempt at sucking up to her ass.

I peered at Angus. He sat diagonally opposite me in the limo. It was the furthest we could be in such a confined space. He just stared out the tinted window. Thank fuck, I hadn't broken his nose, but by the black and bluish color spreading to his eyes, he was in a world of pain. *Good.*

On the jet, he'd apologized, but I knew Jamie had forced him to. He knew he was down to his last roll of the dice, so he didn't fucking dare look me in the eye.

After what he'd said, I didn't feel a shred of remorse. The irony was I was more in control than I'd ever been. I wasn't drunk or womanizing. Being pissed at Angus' outrageous comment drove my fist into his face, nothing else. But the tabloids didn't see it that way. They never saw it my way.

My phone buzzed, and my heart skipped at the thought of it being her. When I flipped it over and saw the head of the record label's name come up, I deflated.

"It's Elliott Cambridge," I announced to the car.

"Oh fuck, Kit." Ryan stiffened in his seat. Jamie and Angus both looked at me, scared as roosters at a roadside stop.

I ignored them and swiped up. "Elliot. How's it going?"

"Not so well, my friend. I just got off the phone with Marcie."

"It's all sorted… just a misunderstanding."

"I thought that's why you fucked off to Seaview. To escape these misunderstandings." His voice was eerily calm —his meaning deadly serious.

"It was." I cleared my throat. "It is."

Nobody fucked with the president of the record label. Even me. When Drew had taken a heap of pills and lay unconscious in a hospital bed, I still hadn't had the courage to stand up to him.

He'd convinced me to stay on tour. We were midway through our European tour when I got the call about my brother. I'd asked Elliot for a release and to cancel the rest of the tour. He refused. Drew would pull through, he'd said, and I fucking believed him.

I didn't have the guts to man up, leave the tour, and return home. Drew died two days later. I didn't even get the chance to say goodbye. All because of Elliot. The man could make or break your career in under a minute. He was the Anna Wintour of music, ruthless as fuck.

He'd done that with the band, Fifty Penny. Then, one day, they'd just disappeared. No more air time, zero promotion, and I'd heard they couldn't even get signed to another label. Not one fucking label would have them. And they were the top ten Billboard and Grammy winners. From sky-high to nobodies overnight. Yeah. No one fucked with Elliot Cambridge.

"Can we have a week in the paper where we don't see your pretty-boy face?"

I knew it wasn't a question.

"Yes, Elliot. Got it."

The phone went dead, and I exhaled. *Fuck him.* My vein throbbed in my neck. Even though we were so fucking successful with tens of millions of dollars in the bank, we were still puppets on a string.

"Well? Do we still have a record deal?" Ryan widened his bloodshot eyes.

"Of course, Ryan. Relax."

"Relax? The president of the record label calls, who might I add, has ties with the New York Mafia, and you tell me to relax! Fuck me." He threw his phone, and it bounced off the leather seats. I shook my head, feeling the weight of the world on my shoulders yet again.

The gate opened, and we drove down the long winding driveway. It was late afternoon, and between the club and travel, I was beat. Regardless of the lack of sleep, the first thing I needed to do was change, then grab a car, and drive to Jazzie's apartment.

"Let's just chill tonight, boys, and start fresh tomorrow." Jamie looked from Angus to me.

"Cool," I said. At this point, all I could think about was Jazzie.

"Sounds good to me." Angus hopped out of the car and headed for the house.

The dickwad could be replaced in my sleep, and he knew it. Angus Turner just cracked his last hailstone.

Jamie and Ryan turned to me, and Jamie put his arm on my shoulder. *Here we go.*

"Kit, we've worked too damn hard to screw this up over a fucking drummer."

"No one talks about Drew like that, Jamie." I flared my nostrils and cracked my bruised knuckles. "No fucking one."

"I get it, bud, but come on, try to stay in control. For us."

If it weren't Angus, it would be someone else who triggered me over Drew. I needed to learn how to deal with it. Although I didn't know how.

I nodded.

I picked up a warm Danish from the kitchen counter and wandered past the hallway into my suite. Thank fuck it was on the other side from Angus' room. At least I could avoid him until studio time tomorrow.

When I pushed open my door, I had to do a double-take. Red hair spread across my pillow, her lips the color of pink roses, and her eyes were closed like that of a sleeping temptress.

My heart swelled.

I slid in beside her, and she stirred, her eyes opening slowly.

"I must have fallen asleep." Sleepily, she lifted her head.

"Hey, red," I said, pressing my lips to hers.

She kissed me back. Her warm lips made the last twenty-four hours disappear.

She pulled away, and I wanted her back. "I heard what happened in Vegas. I thought you might need me."

"Damn tabloids." I slid next to her. Her lavender and rose scent filled my nostrils.

"No. Gregory told me the real deal... what Angus said."

"Angus is a cocksucker." Hearing his name, my hand balled into a fist.

"Why would Angus say something like that to you?" she asked, her voice soft and calm like a drug.

"Because he's right about Drew anyway. I didn't make the right decision. I could have saved him."

"He had his own demons, Kit. There wasn't anything you could do for him."

"I could have been there. I should have flown back to see him while he was unconscious." I groaned, sitting up. "You just don't know, Jazzie. I'm a fucking awful man."

"What are you talking about?" Her hand circled my back, but it did nothing to soothe me.

"I didn't try hard enough to come back to see him. I asked only once. Once, for a release from the tour. He was still alive. I could've made it back. I could have talked to him. I could have convinced him to cling to the threads of life he had left. But no. I was too fucking scared. I lacked the courage to stand up to my label."

"But you said you asked for a release?"

"Asking Elliot Cambridge for a release was like asking his holiness to share a joint. I knew his answer before I even picked up the goddamn phone."

"Why didn't you push then?"

"Because I chose this life over protecting him."

She opened her mouth to speak, but nothing followed. *Now you know I'm a piece of shit, and now I'll lose you too.*

"If I weren't famous and living in New York City, Drew would still be here. With me."

"You don't really think your success resulted in his downfall?"

"I neglected him. I couldn't protect him. Just like I can't protect you, Jazzie."

"What do you mean? You're not making sense, Kit."

I stroked her cheek. Fear and confusion filled her eyes.

14

JASMINE

My hand circled his back, but I'm not sure it had the calming effect I'd hoped for. He'd chosen the life of a rock star over his brother. I should run out the door at his selfish admission, but I didn't see him that way. Far from it.

Crippled with defeat, his eyes were tinged red, and his head hung low. Although exhausted, having him this close flipped my stomach into my throat.

He lifted his head, the back of his hand stroked my cheek, and a wave of heat smacked me between my legs.

"I don't know what this is, red. All I know is I can't stop thinking about you, and it scares the living shit out of me."

I can't stop thinking about you too, I wanted to say the words, but something stopped me.

"I'm here, Chris. That's all I can give you now."

"I know. Please just stay." He closed the gap between us and kissed me with an earth-shattering intensity. My hands found his hair at the same time his lips traced my neck. He rolled onto his knees, facing me, as he flung off his shirt. His torso was like going off-road, each muscle ripped and tight. I ran my fingers down his herculean body, tracing each ripple down to his V.

He shivered, and a wave of heat rolled over my skin, knowing I had this effect on him.

I began unbuckling his belt when he placed a hand on mine.

"No, you first." His commanding voice made me weak in the knees.

I wriggled out of my leggings and daisy pattern underwear as his hands felt underneath my T-shirt, lifting it over my head.

I clenched my thighs, absorbing every inch of his tongue, circling the swell of my breast.

"Fuck! I want all of you." He breathed and ripped off my bra, but I didn't fucking care for it. I needed him inside me, *now*.

Kisses peppered down my belly, onto my hip bone, his possessive touch warming my entire body. Pleasurable soft bites on my upper thighs sent me to almost an orgasm as he spread me apart. His tongue danced between my thighs, languid strokes lavishing me with long strokes.

I threw my head back in pleasure and let out a throaty groan.

He massaged inside me with his fingers, interchanging strokes with his tongue in perfect synchronicity. The sound of my wetness echoed around the room. My skin prickled and hummed as I thrust my hips against him, feeling every inch of his tongue.

I pressed my thighs together, trying to absorb the earthquake building inside me. My heart pounded so loud I was sure he could hear it.

"Come, red," he commanded, hooking his fingers so deep inside me.

My hands balled into fists, unable to withstand the pleasure any longer. His command was my undoing.

"Christopher," I moaned his name as my body convulsed into tsunami-like waves of pleasure.

When my eyes flickered open, he was standing naked and hard at the foot of the bed. "Fuck, you're gorgeous when you come."

"Let me return the favor." I peeled myself off the bed and took him in my hands, stroking him. His impossibly long length extended even more with every stroke.

He threw his head back and sucked in a breath.

"You don't have to do this." He inhaled a sharp breath as I gripped him tighter.

But I wanted him so badly. I wanted to please him, to take his mind off everything. Desire pooled inside me, and there wasn't anything more I wanted at this minute.

"I want to." I wrapped my mouth around him, taking him from tip to base.

"Fuck, red!" he hissed out, his voice filled with equal parts pain and pleasure. Gently, he placed his hands in my hair, guiding me into a gratifying rhythm.

"I want to see you," he said and lifted me onto his hips in one ridiculous athletic move that caught me completely off guard.

"Shit!"

"I got you, baby."

His dark eyes, thick with desire, bored into mine as he leveled me onto him. His hands pressed into my ass, and as he entered me, I gripped his broad shoulders, my hands snaking around his neck.

"I could bathe in your delicious cunt all day long." His dirty words made me groan in ecstasy.

We moved together as he filled me repeatedly. Every nerve ending was alive and screamed for his touch.

"Fuck, Kit." *What was happening to me?* I didn't have time to make sense of it, his touch overloading my body and mind, liquifying any thoughts I might have. He took one of my bobbing breasts into his mouth and sucked it. Hard.

"Chris, shit." I threw my head back. Needles of pleasure pulsed through me.

He tilted my face down to his. "Eyes on me, red. I want to see you come."

I flicked my eyes open, leveling on his brown eyes thick with desire.

My thighs gripped him like glue. His eyes, breath, and fullness inside me became my undoing. With his gaze excruciatingly hot and sensual, I found my release.

He thrust his hips into me again. "Fuck, red." He moaned, closing his eyes and finding his own.

* * *

I lay awake for what seemed like hours, watching the color of the room change from gray to tangerine as day broke. So many times, I wanted to sneak out and drive home, but a force willed me to stay. Lying beside him felt so right, even though it was so very wrong.

He lay on his side, his myriad of tattoos on display. A lion's head, tree roots, Sanskrit letters, and the loops of an infinity symbol were artworks. All inked on his arm. I wondered what they all meant to him and if, one day, he'd tell me.

His soft and low breathing fell on my shoulder like a whisper. He'd fallen asleep after our explosive encounter last night. Kit was unlike anything I'd ever experienced, and it rattled me how much I needed him. I'd never wanted anyone so much in my life before he'd shown up on the scene.

He stirred next to me as the sun peeked higher, casting its shadow on the wall.

I stared at the ceiling, the same ceiling I'd been staring at for hours. *If Kit Jones was a playboy and womanizer, what was I doing with him?*

I turned my head and brushed his nose with my own. His olive complexion and full lips were a sin, tempting me even after I'd been satisfied more than ever before.

I was beyond confused. In my heart, I knew I could never trust him, but what if… *what if it was possible?*

What if Chris could be the one in my plus one? It sounded impossibly true. My stomach lurched like a ride at a carnival, lodging in my throat.

"Hello, beautiful." His voice was a lullaby. He opened his thickly lashed eyes. "Aren't you a mirage?"

I laughed. "I hope your lyrics are better than your corny one-liners."

Immediately his eyes widened. "Is that a challenge, red?"

I flicked my hair from my eyes. "No, absolutely not!"

He grinned, "There are so many things I could write about you."

I blushed from my toes to my scalp, my teeth digging into my bottom lip.

"You are adorable when you blush." He tilted my chin to him, brushing his lips against mine in a dominant kiss that woke up my lady parts.

After a beat, he pulled away abruptly. "Shit, what's the time?"

He bolted upright, checking his chunky gold watch he'd left on the nightstand. "Fuck, it's eight thirty!" He ran his hand through his just-been-fucked bed hair, the same hair I tugged while screaming his name last night. "I can't believe I slept for that long!"

"God, I'm so late," I said, throwing the sheet off my naked body.

"Where are you going?" He reached over and slapped my bare butt.

"I've got to go home, get my camera, and come back here in under thirty minutes."

"Why don't you take a day off today?"

"That's nice and all, but you don't pay my bills." *That didn't come off right.* "Nor would I want you to." Shit, *that didn't sound any better. Quit it, Jazzie.*

"Thanks for the clarification. I'm not saying take the day off completely. Come into the studio, listen to us, and don't worry about any photos today."

Kit's face flooded my camera. I'd taken over two thousand photos of him and the band, so I could probably go without a day of taking any more.

"Only problem with that plan is my co-worker would be wondering why I'm not doing my job."

"Harry. I forgot about that little prick. You know he fancies you, right?"

"A long time ago—"

"Maybe, I could promise him that one-on-one interview he's been pestering me about."

"That could work. He'll still wonder why I'm without my camera. Harry is an investigative journalist, after all."

Kit rubbed his well-kept stubble, a grin spreading into his cheeks. "Do you trust me?"

I twisted my lips. "You know I can't."

He frowned. "Just get ready for the day here. Don't go home."

"But—"

He walked over and pressed his fingers to my lips, preventing me from arguing back. "It will be fine." He smiled, then walked toward the ensuite, which was bigger than my bedroom. His naked body glimmered in the morning light like a modern-day inked Adonis.

It was hard to resist him in the shower, so I didn't. He caged me against the wall and kissed me as though he was breaking a fast. His need for me was insatiable, and it was difficult not to lose myself completely. He pinned me against the wall, sinking into me deeper, and I absorbed every inch of him until I saw stars. Fuck, he was the best lover I'd ever had—selfless, dominant, passionate—hands-fucking-down outrageously perfect. After we regained our breaths, he sauntered out of the shower butt naked like the rock star he was.

* * *

I pressed the shower lever to off as the constant ringing of a phone sounded from the bedroom.

"Chris?" I yelled out but didn't get a reply.

I walked out with a towel wrapped around my hair and body. I'd heard the melodic chime of his phone by the time I'd stepped out, but he wasn't there. After a minute, his phone lit up again on the nightstand. The screen flashed, then stopped. I picked it up, finding four missed calls from the same person. Someone named *Carmel*.

I shivered, my warm body immediately losing heat. Amber, the know-it-all, had mentioned the name Carmel as someone he'd dated. But he'd told me he didn't date. *Had that been a lie?*

The phone rang again. I ran into the bathroom and slammed the door behind me.

I didn't want to know about an ex-girlfriend. Maybe he'd caught up with her in Vegas. A million scenarios swirled in my head as constriction gripped my throat.

"Jazzie, you ready?" The low tone of his voice sang through the bathroom door where I hid.

Sucking in a deep breath, I flung the door open.

"You okay?"

Yes. No, I don't know. I swallowed. "Your phone was ringing."

He paused then walked over to his phone. "Okay, thanks."

I watched him, his face, for any clue as to what he was thinking.

"Someone important?" My jaw twitched.

He slid his phone into his back jean pocket. "The most important person is standing right in front of me. Now come on, I have something for you. As much as I want to unwrap that wet towel off you and spread you apart with my mouth, I have to be in the studio. Meet me by the pool in five? I have a surprise for you."

"Um, sure." *I sounded like a hot mess.*

He flashed his perfectly straight teeth and shut the door behind him. I flopped onto the bed. *See, it was nothing. She's no one.*

I sandwiched my hands together. *He has only ever been honest with me. Don't let your past dictate your future.* Determined to stay positive, I pushed away all thoughts about who Carmel, the devil-woman, could be and reached for my clothes. Washed and ironed by magic laundry fairies, my leggings and T-shirt were hung in Kit's wardrobe.

I ran my fingers through my hair, realizing my makeup was back in my apartment. I shrugged. It wasn't that big of a deal.

True to his word, Kit sat by the pool with his back to the house. I walked up and placed my hands on his shoulders.

"This is for you." He rested his hand on mine, then

guided me around to sit beside him. In front of me, a square red box with a big silver bow sat on the table.

"It's not my birthday," I said, smiling and running my hand across the gloss paper.

"I know. Your birthday is on Valentine's Day."

"How do you k—"

"Just open it," he commanded.

I let out an over-the-top sigh. "Bossy!"

"You love it, red."

I did.

I undid the bow, then carefully unpeeled the wrapping paper.

"Just rip it!" he said, launching in and tearing the other side.

"What the hell?" I tried to comprehend what my fingers were holding onto.

"Well? Do you like it? I was told it's the best."

I stared at the box. It was the best camera on the market. This was the dream camera, the one I'd always wanted but could never afford. A river of joy bubbled through my veins. "Chris, how did you…" I held up a hand to my mouth in disbelief at what was in front of me.

"You needed a camera." He shrugged like he'd just shouted me a coffee instead of dumping twenty thousand on a camera.

Warmth tinged my entire skin. "I won't say I can't accept it, but I will say a million and one thank-yous."

"Thank fuck. I was afraid your fiery streak would get in the way of accepting it."

I laughed. "You know me too well. As much as I would want to hand it back, I couldn't possibly. I've wanted this camera from the moment my passion for landscape photography kicked in. How did you do this? It's nine in the morning, not to mention impossible to get this model in Seaview."

"You can do anything if you splash enough cash around."

I pushed out my chair and climbed onto his lap, placing my hands around his neck. "Thank you."

He pulled me closer, his scent invading my senses. "It's nothing."

I held his face in my hand. "That's not true."

His brows creased together. "Okay, it's something. I've never wanted to please a girl like I have you, red."

My shoulders dropped at his admission. Unable to find any words that could match his, I pulled him close, taking my lips to his.

"Jazzie, I think I want to go to Drew's memorial tomorrow. Will you come with me?"

My heart swelled. "Of course."

15

KIT

It was a small intimate gathering at my parents' home. Mom, Dad, their closest friends, and some of Drew's old mates all gathered on the lawn near the boathouse. Ryan and Jamie had even shown up. I listened to them recount their memories of my twin. One after another, they stood with the ocean as their backdrop, and I absorbed every moment, letting their fond memories of him wash over me.

The keen surfer, the joker, the all-around nice guy. These thrown-around words in countless conversations described my brother to the core.

Dad walked out from beyond the small crowd, stepping up onto the rock ledge bordering the memorial garden they'd planted in Drew's honor. Hundreds of flowers swayed in the ocean breeze. Blue and yellow forget-me-nots, lilac and white daisies, and rounded rosemary bushes colored Drew's memorial garden.

"What kind words you all have had for Drew. My son was all those things. I only wished he viewed himself that way. But his demons were far greater than any one of us could have possibly imagined, and they eventually took him from us."

His weathered eyes brimmed with tears. "It was no one's fault. No one was to blame." Dad turned to me, and my chest tightened, the weight of a thousand rocks stealing the breath from my lungs.

"Gone too young and too soon, Drew's spirit lives on. He lives on in you, Christopher."

Jazzie squeezed my hand tighter as tears pricked in the corner of my eyes.

"He was always so proud of you, son. He loved you so much."

Dad took a few steps toward me. Each step he took, my heart pounded louder and harder. "Drew lives on in you." His hand rested on my shoulder. "Honor him every day by being the best man you can."

A tear escaped the corner of my eye, and Dad pulled me in for a hug. I let him. I breathed in, letting go of the guilt that I'd shouldered for a year, feeling all of Dad's love and all of Drew's love from above. It beat down on me like the eternal warmth of the sun.

Dad patted me on the back, then turned to the guests.

"Thank you all for coming. There's food up at the house. Let's share more stories of Drew while we drink to the memory of my son."

I remained while everyone else set off toward the house. Vacantly, I stared at the ocean. Eerily flat and calm, it appeared like a sheet of glass. Jazzie sat on the sandstone boulder beside me, her silence not in the slightest bit uncomfortable. During the entire memorial, she'd wrapped her hand in mine, never once removing it. After some time, I turned to her. She was more beautiful than anyone I'd ever known—milky white skin, a dusting of freckles on her cheeks, and almond-shaped eyes like flawless diamonds—

perfect. Suddenly, being here with her, I realized my heart would be incomplete without her.

But I saw her wounds. They cut deep like mine. If only I could hold her and tell her I'd be there for her. I was beginning to believe it, too, now. I could be the man she needed. I had to believe in that, or I would lose her forever. I stared, getting lost in her emeralds.

"Are you okay?" Jazzie whispered.

"I am. I'm actually right where I ought to be."

She smiled, her rose lips turning up into a heart-touching smile. "I'm glad you came."

"So am I." I exhaled. *If I didn't ask her now, then when?* "Jazzie, would you consider coming back with me to New York?"

She pulled at her copper hair, her flashbulb eyes huge. "Really?"

I nodded. "Really, Jazzie."

"Chris, that's a huge decision. This has been crazy fast."

"I know it is, but doesn't it feel so right?" I exhaled. I've never been so certain about anything in my life. "Can you promise me you'll think about it?"

She blinked rapidly, her hands turning clammy as they palmed mine. "Okay."

"Jasmine, Christopher?" Mom's voice billowed from the balcony.

"Here, Ma," I yelled as she made her way back down the tiered steps to us.

She smiled at Jazzie, then me. "Will you come up to the house? Ryan and Jamie want to know where their buddy is."

I smiled. "Coming, Ma." Reluctantly, I let go of Jazzie's hand and headed toward the house.

"Go on, Chris. You two can have more smoochy time

later. I'll keep your seat warm." She squished my cheeks before I leaned away from her, laughing.

"Ma, who the fuck says smoochy?" I turned my head.

"Language, Christopher!"

Ma had perched herself in my seat next to a giggling redhead who had stolen my heart.

* * *

I trudged into the house. Jamie and Ryan were hovering around the food table, chatting to Jasper and Kelso, friends of Drew's.

"Hey, Kit," Jasper said as I approached them. "Nice service."

"Yeah, it was, actually." I shook his hand, noticing he'd hardly changed and was still every bit the baby-faced, scruffy blond surfer friend of Drew's.

"I miss my friend so much, but I look at you and see so much of him in you."

"They were twins," Ryan said flatly.

"Shut up, Ryan." Jaime pushed his elbow into his ribs.

Jasper ignored Ryan's attempt to lighten the mood. "I know you were not identical. You feel me, Kit, yeah?"

"I do. Thanks, man, for coming."

"Bro, if you ever need anything, I'm here for you. Jasper and I both are," Kelso said, slapping me on the back.

"Thanks, and same here. I'm sorry I haven't been there for you both over the last year," I said, knowing I should have reached out to his two best friends.

"Well, you have every excuse, Mr. Highflyer," Kelso said.

"I can still pick up a phone," I admitted.

"No, we have people who do that for us now," Ryan quipped, and we dissolved into laughter.

"You can count on hearing from me from now on, boys," I said, shaking both their hands with a firm grip.

* * *

We hovered in the chopper high above the city. Jamie and Ryan stared vacantly at their phones, and Jazzie took in the scenery. I reached for my phone in my pocket, realizing it had been on silent the entire day.

Fuck, seven missed calls from Carmel.

She'd been my fuck buddy until recently. A party a week before we left was thrown in honor of us reaching number one practically worldwide. She'd come up to me after I was beyond wasted and ended up in my bed. What turned out to be a party ended up being a three-day bender of gigantic proportions.

Why couldn't she move on from that?

I shoved the phone back in my pocket and glanced over at Jasmine, her hair parted neatly underneath the headset. I couldn't work out what she was thinking.

Maybe she was confused about the invite to New York. I guess it wasn't every day she got an invitation like that.

My phone buzzed again. I slid it out to switch the damn thing off. Carmel was right well pissing me off now. Instead, a text cornered me.

Carmel: *Answer your phone, Kit. I'm pregnant.*

The floor disappeared from underneath me, and I was free-falling to Earth. My heart rate spiked, and all the air in the helicopter wasn't nearly enough. My airways started closing, crushing every last sap of air.

No. Fuck, no!

I wanted to scream.

I looked around. Jazzie gazed out the window, Jamie too. Ryan arched a brow. "It looks like you've seen a ghost. You okay, bud?"

Now everyone was staring at me. I couldn't show anything. I couldn't say a goddamn thing.

I nodded, dead inside.

"Fine, just air sick."

"Since when?" Jamie asked.

"Since fucking now, all right?" I snapped back.

"Whoa, chill out," Jamie said, staring back out the window.

Jazzie placed her hand on my knee. "Is there anything I can do to help?"

"No," I said, sucking in a few deep lungfuls of air.

Definition of fucked. Getting a one-night stand fucking pregnant if you're a rock star. I felt sick to my stomach.

* * *

I pushed Jazzie away, asking her to leave and go home on the pretense that I wasn't feeling well.

I knew she saw straight through it, but I couldn't tell her the truth. Not until I knew for certain this wasn't some cruel fucking joke.

I dialed her number, not giving a shit what time it was on the East Coast.

"I thought you'd call." Carmel's voice was laden with sarcasm. She was a kinky fuck. That I remembered, but I couldn't remember if I'd strapped on a rubber.

"Carmel. Are you sure it's mine?"

"Fuck you, Kit."

"Okay, okay," I said, kicking the ottoman on the floor. It flew halfway across the room, crashing into a light.

"What was that?"

"Nothing."

"Kit, it's yours. I took a test because I was late."

I sighed. All my recklessness was bound to catch up with me someday. Today was it.

"Say something," she said.

"I have nothing to say."

It's fucking over.

"I want this child, Kit."

Like you want a few more extra zeros in your bank account.

"It was just a one-time thing, Carmel. Fuck, I don't even know your last name."

"It's Stinger. I know we just fucked, Kit. I'm under no illusion we'll be together."

"Good," I said, probably a little too quickly.

"Jesus, thanks."

"Fuck, Carmel, let me just process this, all right?"

Dad's words rang in my ear, *"Be the honorable man I know you can be."*

"I'll be there to support you and the child. I won't let you down."

"I know you will. When are you back?"

"I've got another week here, but we're ahead of schedule. Just do me a favor, Carmel, stay quiet about this. Please."

"Yeah, yeah, I know the press would cream their panties over this scoop."

"Carmel!" I yelled.

"All right, chill." She laughed, but there was nothing funny about it.

* * *

My second call was to Robert, my lawyer, who said he'd liaise with Carmel. Apparently, she was expecting their call. I guess she knew having Kit's baby equaled payday. So speaking with a lawyer would be the start of that conversation.

I sat down, scotch in hand. The drink was soothing my frayed nerves.

"Fellas, I've got someone pregnant."

Jamie dropped the pool cue onto the tiled floor.

"You fuckwit, why didn't you wear a rubber?" Ryan threw his hands on his head.

Like it was their fucking problem!

"Is it Jazzie?" Angus asked, still not meeting my eyes.

I wish.

"No, it's not," I said. Angus always had an opinion on fucking everything.

"Who then?" Jamie asked.

"Do you remember before we left the States, the party over at the Standard?"

"No, not that blonde woman with the shorts that just covered her snatch?" Ryan asked.

"Yeah, her."

"I knew the second I saw her she was fucking trouble, Kit," Jamie said. "I think I even tried to tell you that, but you were too shit-faced to even know which way was up."

I threw back the scotch. The dark liquid burned down my throat.

"Well, it's mine. She's having it, and that's that." I slammed down the glass.

"What does this mean?" Ryan asked.

"I'm going back to New York tomorrow. We all are. We can finish the single back there."

"And Jazzie?" Jamie asked.

"I haven't told her. I'm hoping she will come with me."

Angus laughed. "You're dreaming. A small-town girl chasing after a rock star." He shook his head.

"I don't see it either, my friend, and I really like Jazzie," Ryan said.

"Sorry," Jamie added.

"Will she keep her mouth shut?" Angus asked.

"Yes, I've got my lawyer on it."

"Thank fuck," Angus said, picking up a cue and breaking the stack. He and Ryan hovered around the table, sinking ball after ball.

I looked at the bottle of scotch, tempted by her numbing abilities. But now more than ever, I needed to be clear-headed.

Jamie sat down on the couch beside me. "I'm sorry, man."

My eyes leveled on the floor as anguish settled in my stomach. "It's my fault."

"Nah, she had you pegged the moment she laid eyes on you."

"Can't you convince her not to have it?"

"I probably could, but I won't."

"Why? You're twenty-five, in the prime of your fucking life. If you think you can, why don't you at least try?" Confusion etched on his black brow.

I shook my head. "You won't get it."

"Try me."

I exhaled. "All this time, I've felt guilty about not being able to protect Drew. I've blamed myself for his death. Now I'm fucked. I either lose the girl I love or lose my unborn child. I just can't protect the ones I love."

He slouched back in his chair, his eyes wide. "You love Jazzie?"

I nodded. "Yeah, man. I didn't realize it until today at the memorial."

"Fuck me." He scratched his head. "And this baby? You sure you won't convince her not to have it?"

I nodded. "Yes."

Without putting it off anymore, I got out my phone and texted Jazzie.

Me: *Can you meet me at the house at seven thirty tomorrow?*

A moment later, my phone pinged.

Jazzie: *Sure. You okay?*

Hell no.

Me: *Yes.*

I hit send and swallowed the lump in my throat.

16

JASMINE

I've fallen for a rock star. Head over heels, crazy, crush-worthy fallen. The worst kind. The type I swore I'd never get involved with—the kind you never want to bring home to meet your parents—especially mine.

Yesterday, at Drew's memorial service, he'd let go of all the guilt that plagued him and completely opened up to me. My ex, who I'd been with for two years, had never been so transparent the entire time we were together. Kit trusted me implicitly.

But I'd be lying if I said I wasn't afraid. Terrified, actually. He'd asked me to move to New York to be with him, and I didn't have an answer. I hadn't even told Amber or Lily. I couldn't. They'd simply laugh at me. If it didn't feel so real, I'd probably laugh too. So outlandish and quick, it just seemed too good to be true.

I pulled up to the iron gates, my stomach swarming with butterflies. Was it such an outrageous idea, him and me, that it could actually work? The gardens were lush green, manicured to an inch of a leaf. The sprinklers danced in the morning sun, and the birds chirped like no one was listening. I shook my head. *This couldn't be my reality, could it?*

Gregory greeted me as he opened my car door. "Jazzie! Good morning! You're here early."

"Yes, it *is* a good morning. And, yes, I am. Chris… I mean, Kit wanted me here early."

His smile beamed north, but he didn't say anything.

Strolling through the cottage, its size and scale still astounded me. Why did they even call it a cottage? It was the exact opposite, resembling more like an Italianate mansion.

Gently, I tapped on Chris' door, aware he may still be sleeping. After all, Drew's memorial was an emotional day. I opened the door when I didn't hear a reply.

But he was sitting at the foot of the bed, staring into space.

"Hey, Jazzie," he said, blinking when his gaze landed on mine.

"Hey." I took him in—his face was tight and dark circles hovered below his strained eyes.

"You okay, Chris? You look like you haven't slept a wink."

Slowly, he walked toward me, brushed his lips against mine, and wrapped his arms around me, pulling me into a tight embrace. He felt warm, and I became desperate for his touch. I deepened the kiss, and he kissed me back, our breaths growing shorter as we craved one another. Abruptly, he pulled back, removing his hands from my hypnotized body. Disappointment reigned.

"Jazzie, please sit."

My stomach knotted into balls, but I did as he asked.

"There's no studio work today, and you're right. I didn't sleep a wink," he replied.

"Well, Drew's memorial would have been draining. Plus, you didn't look well last night. I should have stayed with you."

His gaze drifted to the floor, and I got this sinking feeling in the pit of my stomach.

"Jazzie, we're flying back to New York today."

I surveyed the room, anything but meeting his gaze. By the entrance were two neatly packed suitcases I walked straight past.

"Why?" I asked, my voice shaky.

"I've never lied to you, and I'm not about to start now."

He got up and started pacing the suite. Suddenly, my head ached, and my stomach twisted into knots.

"Before we left New York, we were partying in Manhattan, one last hurrah before leaving and coming to Seaview. It was an epic night with celebrities, models, basically, anyone who's anyone showed up to celebrate with us." He raked his hand through his hair. "At this party, I slept with a woman. I was drunk, reckless, and don't remember much of it, to be completely honest with you."

"Why are you telling me this?" My voice returned. Imagining him with anyone but me suddenly made me insanely jealous.

He turned around, his eyes dark and serious. "Because she's pregnant."

My skin crawled, and my stomach churned. All I could do was sit there and take it like a bullet train. Was I the ongoing joke in a bad comedy? *The one that always got fucked over.*

"Jazzie, did you hear me?"

I cleared my throat. "Predictable."

"What?"

"What did I expect? From the moment I saw someone

on their knees at the karaoke bar to now this. I don't know why I thought we could be anything else."

"Because we can, Jazzie." He stepped closer toward me, reaching out to touch me.

I stepped back. "No."

His eyes widened, "This was all before I met you. This doesn't change things."

I laughed. *Was he fucking serious?*

"I don't even know Carmel."

Fuck. The name on his phone.

"We aren't together. It was a one-time thing. I was dumb, off my head, and didn't wear a rubber."

"See, predictable." With all the pull on Earth, I held back the tears that threatened the back of my eyes. I straightened and held my head high. "We would have never worked anyway, Kit."

"Kit? So now we're back to Kit?" Again, he reached for my hand, and I pulled it away. "Just please listen to me," he pleaded, anguish strewn across his handsome face.

I couldn't bear it anymore. I stepped further away and turned toward the door.

"Stop, Jazzie. Don't you get it? I love you."

His outburst rendered me to a stop. I turned around, his brown eyes wide, sincere as the declaration he'd just made. "I've never loved anyone in my life, and it scares the hell out of me. We can work this stuff out with the baby. Just please, come with me to New York."

I breathed in and out, feeling at any moment my heart could burst out of my chest.

He stepped in closer, "Please, just trust me."

I sucked in a shaky breath. A tear escaped and rolled down my cheek.

Maybe I don't deserve love after all.

"You know I can't." I opened the door and walked out

of Kit's room, running out of the double doors, past Paula in the kitchen and Gregory in the foyer.

Kit shouted my name, but I kept running to the safety of my car. I turned the key, slammed it into gear, and accelerated the hell out of there.

I was in my head the entire drive home. So much so I didn't realize I was sitting in my car outside my apartment. *How long had I been here for?*

Switching off the engine, I climbed out. I flung myself up the flight of stairs, just managing to get to the top before my legs gave out. Out of breath and exhaling, I wiped away the flood of tears.

The key slid into the barrel, and the lock clicked open. The second I opened the door had to be the moment I shut him out completely—the curve of his face, the depth of sincerity in his chocolate eyes, fingering the short hairs on his chest, and how my body responded to his touch. They were all things of the past.

I slammed the door shut behind me. The sunlight streamed in from the ocean into the living room. My legs barely carried me to my room, and I collapsed onto the unmade bed, burying my head underneath my pillow.

* * *

"Jazzie, your phone has been ringing off the hook. Just answer it, would you?"

Amber's voice shook me out of my lucid dreams. My stinging eyes widened, taking in the darkened room. *Shit, what was the time?*

"Jazzie! Get your butt out here."

"Coming! Quit your yelling." I flung the quilt off and ran out of my room, the sound of a phone like a drill hammer. "Where is it?"

"There." Amber lay on the couch, pointing to my phone dancing across the table an arm's length away from her.

"Gee, thanks."

"You're welcome," she said without diverting her eyes from the magazine she had in her grasp.

Just as I picked up my phone, it stopped ringing. "Shit." Fred's name, like a migraine, flashed on my screen seven times.

"Whoa, you okay?" Amber lifted her attention, studying my face.

Death probably appeared more attractive.

"Yes," I lied.

"You look like shit."

"Wow. Thanks."

"Was that Kit calling you?" she asked.

Just hearing his name seared a hole in my chest. "No. Fred."

"Why is he calling you after hours?"

"Probably because I didn't show up for work today."

She dropped the magazine in her lap. "And why not?"

I pressed his name. "Let me call him before I lose my job completely. Then you have to spring me for the rent."

"Go then." She waved her hands, ordering me away, then returned her attention to her magazine.

I stepped outside onto the balcony. The humidity smacked me in the face, despite the low-slung sun.

"Where the fuck have you been, Jasmine?"

Great. "Hi, Fred."

"Well?"

He wasn't having any of it. "I turned up today at the cottage, then got the news. Four Fingers was returning to New York, so I came home."

"And what makes you think you can go home?" he snapped.

I sighed. "I just thought you wouldn't have anything for me today."

"Are you hearing yourself?"

"Well, to be honest, I've put in so much overtime that I'm owed at least a day off."

"And you thought you could simply pick and choose when to take that? I expect all the photos you took of Kit and the band first thing Monday." The line went dead.

Fuck.

* * *

I'd avoided Amber for the rest of the weekend, locking myself in my room with my laptop and camera, using the old busy-with-work excuse. I'd taken over three thousand photos of the band, but as I sifted through them, I'd realized most of those were of Kit, front and center. Some said I was meticulous and OCD with my work. I'd like to think of it as being thorough. In each photo, his chocolate brown eyes stared into my soul. Painstakingly, I went through each image, touching up and editing my work. Each one squeezed my heart that little more.

The sun lowered on Sunday evening as I admired the photos I'd captured during my time in the cottage.

Exhaustion eclipsed every bone in my body, and the only thing I could do was climb into bed. After placing my phone on the nightstand, sadness washed over me. Kit would have landed in New York City by now, and as much as I wanted to speak to him and check if he was okay, I just couldn't. I'd just been through enough. Heartbreak and I went hand in hand, and there was no point dragging it out. Making it only barely easier was the radio silence from his end as well. No calls or texts. Maybe he'd regretted asking me to move to New York with him. After all, when we met, he'd said he didn't believe in monogamy.

Anger quickly replaced sadness. *Was I naïve to think there could be something between us? Had I not learned a damn thing from my previous screwed-up exes?*

Although this didn't fall into the realm of any previous relationship, I couldn't ignore the fact he moved in different circles than me. Women flocked to him like seagulls to fries. My weak heart wasn't equipped for that pain.

Maybe settling for Mr. Boring rather than Mr. Break-My-Heart would work. It did for my sister, and she seemed happy. I switched off my phone, avoiding the temptation to check it. Tomorrow, the wrath of Fred would rear its head, and to tackle that, I needed sleep and a clear head.

* * *

Fred rounded the table. "Jazzie, these are amazing." He flicked through each photo on my computer quicker than I'd like, but it was all the same to an untrained eye.

"This is your best work yet. You've captured a vulnerability about Kit that has rarely been depicted." He rubbed his hands together. "It's like I see the guy in a whole new light."

"Thanks, Fred." I rolled my lips together. "He's easy to capture."

He stared over the computer screen, giving me that look of his. I didn't know whether or not he was going to tell me off or drill me like a father figure.

"So the rumor is he had to leave suddenly because he's become a baby daddy. Do you know anything about that?"

It wasn't my secret to tell, nor would I ever divulge anything to a journalist. "Why would I?"

He narrowed his wiry eyes. "Harry mentioned Kit took a shining toward you. Now, why do I get the feeling you're not being honest with me, Jasmine?"

I shrugged. "I don't know."

"You know, this could be a real game-changer for you if you knew something."

"I wish I could tell you, but I honestly don't know what you're talking about."

"What's in the envelope?" His tone was curt.

"These are my top five photos. I thought it might help you narrow them down."

"Oh, give me, give me." He snatched the envelope from my grasp.

Releasing them from my hold felt like a personal part of what I had with Kit was now on public record. A tinge of sadness swept over my body.

The grin on his face broadened. "This one. This one is the money shot."

I knew exactly which shot he was talking about. I'd captured him on a break after he'd played a new lyric he'd just written. Standing tall against the studio wall, with sleeves rolled up and his guitar resting on his thigh, his face turned up into a hint of a smile right at the point of shoot. Through the lens, he'd appeared vulnerable, expanded, and real.

"I think we will make a mint out of this. Good job, Jazzie."

"Does that mean I can now choose whatever jobs I want?"

He tucked the photos back into the envelope and laughed. "Sure, what did you have in mind?"

Adrenaline pumped through my veins. Finally. Finally, I had free rein and the permission to do what I loved the most. Countless times I'd dreamed of this day, already jotting down a never-ending list of must-visit landscapes, not only in Australia but around the world.

"I've got it all sorted. We can start locally here in Queensland. Babinda Boulders, the Daintree, and Cape York. Then further interstate, there's Wave Rock. The hundred-yard wall of granite shaped into a crashing wave. Did you know it's over two million years old? Gosh, there are so many. How about the waterfalls of Litchfield National Park, or the—"

He held up his hand. "Hold up." He let out a laugh. "I think you're forgetting something."

"Hang on. There's more, Fred. The twenty-thousand-year-old petroglyphs in Pilbara are meant to be super spectacular."

"Okay. We're getting ahead of ourselves. Did you hit your head on the way to work this morning?"

"Huh?"

"I think you're forgetting we are a newspaper that needs to sell papers."

"I'm not forgetting that, Fred."

"So, why on earth would someone be interested in a fucking wave wall?"

"Well, because how I capture things, as you know, is unique, and that's why you hired me for these specialized jobs. I photograph things with an angle and point of view that is original and fresh."

"Yeah, but at the end of the day, no one's going to pick up and read a story about a rock. People pick up a paper with a headline like, *Kit Jones Impregnates Party Girl.*"

The headline curdled my blood, turning it ice-cold.

"But you said I would have free rein after the band job. It's been four years, Fred!"

"And we aren't *National Geographic,* Jasmine!"

I tossed a strand of hair away that had fallen across my face. *Would this really be the way forward?*

"The next job I have, I think, will interest you. Just take a listen." Fred picked up a document from his desk, but he'd already lost me.

"It's a job out at Brisbane, and it is a falling uninsured skyscraper. I thought you'd enjoy photographing the architecture and the angles."

I exhaled, excitement leaving my body quicker than a burst dam wall. There was no way Fred was giving me what he'd promised. Even after all this time I'd proven myself time and time again. He knew I was the best photographer here, and now, I believed it to be true.

"I can't, Fred."

"What do you mean you can't?"

I stood up. "I don't know what's ahead, but I know it's not this."

"Come on, Jazzie, you know you have a responsibility to me and this newspaper."

I shouldered my backpack. "Thanks, Fred, but this isn't what I want anymore."

"What will your parents say?" He folded his arms as I opened his office door.

"Who cares."

17

KIT

Two weeks ought to be enough time to get over her. But, as I stared out the window on the fifty-second floor on the Upper East Side, the snow fell in a gentle flurry, its beauty a stark reminder of Jasmine.

I envied couples who strolled hand in hand. Doing double-takes at redheads, wishing they were her, had become a regular occurrence. Just about everything reminded me of her, but she'd shut me off like a leaky tap. But with a baby on the way and an upcoming tour, reality whacked me like blunt-force trauma.

Every moment I felt compelled to contact her, to hear her voice on the phone, assuring me everything would be okay, but I held back. I told her I loved her, but even though she hadn't said it back, I knew deep down she felt *something*. It was in the depth of her kiss and her touch. But she was scared, and she'd never trust me. Her past boyfriends closed her off to anything real ever again. I closed my eyes, shutting out New York and the blizzard in my heart.

"Kit, sorry to keep you waiting. Please, come in. I've got the team here." James Penrose, trusted attorney to the stars or whoever could afford his exorbitant fees, extended his arm.

"James." I took his hand, thankful he was aware of everything that had happened the last two weeks.

Many trusted faces, buried in paperwork and conversations, lifted their heads when I entered the boardroom.

"Heya, Kit," Marcie said.

"Hi, Marcie, Joy." They were the team I trusted. Marcie, my miracle public relation's goddess, who spun a terrible story into something positive for my career, and head of marketing for the record label, Joy, sat beside her. She was the brain trust with getting our music out into the market, especially when we had come to New York as newbies.

James offered me the seat at the head of the table while he positioned himself in the seat beside me. Across from him was his team of four ruthless lawyers. I nodded, recognizing a few of them.

Since the news broke around the world that I was to be a baby daddy, tabloids had smashed it about, cashing in on click-bait headlines. They'd hand-painted me in a light that was typical of the womanizer and playboy. The team in front of me had their work cut out.

After only a few days of investigating, a paper trail of payments from a prominent media outlet linked the leak to Carmel. My lawyers had a private eye team of investigators who looked into her. Moonlighting as a server during the day and part-time stripper in the evenings summed her up. "You sure know how to pick 'em," Dad had said when I told him. But it was all just noise, a distraction, and a pull away from my Jazzie.

"Okay, let's begin." James slid his glasses up along the bridge of his pointy nose. "Right, we struck up a deal with Carmel Stinger and her team. I've discussed the details with Kit regarding alimony and her allowance. And because of Kit and his generosity, Carmel has agreed to sign it off."

"I bet she wanted the goddamn kitchen sink. She strikes me as such." Marcie flung a tightly woven curl from her face. Marcie looked like she needed a week in Saint Barts or a client that didn't give her so much grief twenty-four-fucking-seven.

I shrugged, "I don't care about zeros and decimal points, Marcie."

"This is why you need to listen to the best team around you, Kit. Both Robert and James said you could have paid way less than what you agreed. Why did you give her what she wants?"

Robert, the head of the law firm and father of his lawyer son James, cleared his throat. He'd remained pretty quiet until now. "What Mr. Jones wanted and cared about the most was being there for his unborn child. So, we negotiated equal rights and an agreeable visitation schedule so that Mr. Jones could be there in the child's life."

"Really?" Joy widened her eyes, the only thing on her Botox face that still moved.

"Yes, Joy, I want to be there as much as I can."

"You've got a tour coming up soon. Kit, we need to paint you in a better light. The media smashed you this time." Marcie tapped her pencil on the mahogany table.

I fidgeted at the table, wanting to be anywhere but here. I don't even know why I had to be here. I needed to record. Be in the studio. *Anywhere but here.*

"Come to think of it, we could use the photos from your time in Seaview. That photographer Joy booked took some amazing photos of you. A *GQ* or *Vogue* cover could work. We could spin the press and redirect them to your time in Seaview rather than bogged down in the quagmire of today's headlines."

"Jazzie's photos?" I asked.

Marcie glanced at her notepad. "Jasmine Winters, yes."

Hearing her name punched a hole in my artery. "Yeah, she's really talented."

"Okay, let me worry about that. You focus on your music and tour."

"You should hear the new EP, Marcie. It sounds perfect," Joy added.

"Thanks, Joy. I've recorded another three songs as well."

Joy's Botoxed eyebrows raised toward her scalp. "Wait, I'm head of marketing, and I haven't even heard this new stuff. When did you do this?".

"Since I've been back. It's just been me, my guitar, and Cohen in the studio mixing. It's an acoustic set of songs."

"Can we hear it?" Marcie asked.

"Yeah, sure." I dug out my phone from my jeans pocket, inhaled, and suddenly felt nervous. Then, hit play.

Over the next fifteen minutes, I'd kept my head down. Then, remembering her vivid eyes, feisty attitude, and quirky style-dungarees and Converse shoes brought a smile to my lips.

It was the silence in the room that made me realize my songs had finished playing. I lifted my chin, taking in the space around me. Marcie and Joy stared at me like I had three heads.

"What the hell, Kit?" Joy asked.

No one had ever questioned my work, but I realized this differed completely from my normal stuff.

"I'll tell you what it is, Joy. It's a goddamn masterpiece." Marcie beamed.

"Holy shit, Kit, I didn't know you had that in you," Joy said, coming over and planting a kiss on my head.

Awash with silent relief, I admitted, "Neither did I."

"Screw *GQ*, Kit. *This* is it. *This* is what we need. *This* will turn everything around," Marcie exclaimed.

The songs were so personal that sharing them with the world was a step I wasn't sure I could take.

Joy and Marcie spoke over one another, scheming and orchestrating the next move. I raked my hands through my hair. The songs were all about her. For once in my life, I was nervous about what Jazzie would think and what she'd say. Then I remembered she'd practically dared me to write a song about her. Well, I'd definitely done that three times over and had more fuel to write an entire album dedicated to her and our time together.

"Great music, Mr. Jones. Do you mind, though, if we get back to the Carmel issue?" Robert asked.

"As far as I'm concerned, the Carmel issue is dead," Marcie crowed. "These new songs, Kit, will put you into the stratosphere."

I scratched at the stubble on my chin, realizing I hadn't shaved since being back. I peered down at my dirty jeans. Truth was, I really hadn't taken good care of myself at all since leaving Jazzie.

"I'm with Marcie on this, Kit, but I think we should record it as a solo album," Joy suggested. I snapped my head up, annoyed by her input.

"And leave Jamie and Ryan behind. Forget it. I won't do it."

"Even if it means this would put you in the world of

idols who transcend generations, musicians who you absolutely adore?" Joy leaned forward and pressed the pads of her fingers together.

"I don't expect you to understand, Joy, but I grew up with these two guys, and they're straight-up, stand-up Aussie fellas. I'm not going to just throw them out to the wolves. Angus, on the other hand…" I rolled my eyes.

"You're right, I don't get it, but I'll go along with it. Jamie and Ryan are in. Angus… I'll have to sugarcoat that one somehow, but it won't be easy." Joy puffed out her cheeks, exasperated.

"How quickly can we get these songs out there, Joy?" Marcia asked.

"They're pretty polished as it is. I'd say a day or two if we can get you all into the studio straight after this," Joy replied.

"All right, I'm going to work with my team on the release strategy and set up interviews with newspapers, promos, and radio stations, and let's do an acoustic live set in Times Square." Marcie frantically jotted down notes in her notepad and accosted us with her plans.

"Oh yes, perfect. See if you can book it on Valentine's Day."

Fuck. Talk about rubbing salt into the wound.

"Yes," Marcie exclaimed. "Oh, that's perfect."

"Hold up, hold up," I raise both hands in protest. "I'm not sure we should release these."

"Why?" Marcie asked, utterly perplexed by my concern.

"Because they're really personal." They didn't need to know any more. I glanced from Marcie to Joy, then to Robert, who'd rightly kept quiet, not competing with the duo force in front of him.

"As long as this isn't about Carmel, Kit, you should release," Marcie said.

I laughed. "It most definitely is not about *her*."

"Carmel doesn't have red hair," Joy said, the corners of her eyes lifting as she smiled.

"Ah, yes, that line, *'Fire hair and green eyes.'*" Marcie nodded.

Resting my hands on my thighs, I let out a deep exhalation. "You know, let's just do it." Telling the truth of how I felt was just too cathartic not to share.

"Hell yes." Marcie slapped the table. "Get ready to be busy."

Perfect. "A distraction is what I need."

"Really pleasant songs, Kit. I think we're done here. Just sign here and here." James pointed to the lengthy document he slid in front of me.

I signed, relieved to be putting that part behind me.

"I'll let you know when she's signed," James said, his team already dispersing out the door.

Joy turned to Marcie. "When do you think you can get the PR strategy done?"

"I'll get on it now." I'm sure Marcie had already fired off three emails just sitting there. She typed quicker than a court clerk.

Joy bounced on her chair. "We can release a teaser right now. I'll call Cohen and get a snippet up on social media."

My chest heaved as a tingly sensation flooded my body, settling in the bottom of my stomach.

Nerves were so foreign.

Yet here they were.

Why was I so nervous about releasing these?

* * *

I hung up my headphones as Jamie entered the booth.

"Kit, that was truly from the heart, brother."

Jamie and Ryan had recently finished laying down the backup acoustics and harmonies. It was well after midnight, and the three of us and Cohen were still in the studio. Working back-to-back the last two days in the studio meant we'd just finished all three tracks.

"I had no idea you felt that way about her," Ryan said.

"Is it that obvious?"

"The lyrics are too real, man. Are you sure you want this shit out there?" Jamie asked.

"No, but what have I got to lose if I've already lost her?"

"Come on, Kit, it can't be that bad."

"It really is. She wants nothing to do with me. Period. I don't blame her. I have a baby on the way, and I'm in a band that's gallivanting around the world. If that's not baggage, what is?"

"Maybe this is exactly what you need, Kit," Ryan added.

"What, a baby?"

"Well, something that settles you. The baby is a given, but Jazzie, if she's that force in your life, why let her go?"

"It's not up to me. The fact is, I'm finally at peace with Drew. I realized there wasn't anything I could have done to prevent him from doing what he did. But for damn sure, I'm not going to ever leave anyone else unprotected like he must have felt. I won't make the same mistake twice. I'm going to protect my child with everything that I am."

"But that's you, Kit. It's nothing new. You look after everyone and always have." Ryan looked at Jamie, then they leveled their stares at me.

"Marcie told me Joy wanted you to go solo on this

one." He slapped me on the shoulders. "That means so much to us both, Kit."

"Of course, Ry. I wouldn't have it any other way. The three of us are more than friends. I consider you family. Always have. There's no way I'm letting any bullshit come between us like that. Plus, let's face it, I need you guys just as much as you need me." I winked. "You ground me in this fake bullshit celebrity world we live in."

* * *

Jamie looked up from his phone with a cheesy grin. "Ah, so guys, we're booked up."

True to Marcie's word, she gave the song out to everyone and booked us everywhere before the US tour this summer.

"They're likening the new song to a classic Beatles love song." Jamie grinned.

"Oh, how the press has turned," Cohen said. "Kit, I don't know how you do it. Time and time again, you just reinvent yourself. This sound, it's old-school, fresh like vintage blues. This is going to take the world by storm."

I turned to Cohen, unable to comprehend the last few days. "It's crazy. They were the quickest lyrics I'd ever written."

A few moments passed when Cohen spoke again. "Have you ever thought about calling her?"

I exhaled. "No, she's been fucked over so many times, I'm just another guy doing it all over again."

"But you didn't fuck her over," he stated.

"Not intentionally, but finding out I'm going to be a baby daddy changes things."

"Does it, though?" Cohen scratched at his thinning

hairline, and I sat down on the stool with my head in my hands.

"This life isn't for her. She just wants simple and easy, no strings attached."

"What, because that's worked for her so far?" Now, Jamie had the nerve to chime in. "From what you've told me, her love life hasn't exactly been smooth sailing."

I may have divulged some of what Jazzie had told me about her ex to Jamie on the plane.

"If Kit can't get his girl, what hope is there for us, boys?" Jamie questioned.

"I don't know, fellas. I've got so much coming up. She's basically said she wants nothing to do with me." The thought was like a sucker punch to the throat.

Jamie sat cross-legged, hope in his eyes. "Maybe when she hears this song, she'll change her mind?"

"I can't protect her from all the tabloids, media, and shitstorms I'm going to get for the rest of my life. She deserves better."

"How you protect her is by staying true to her," Cohen said.

"Oh, that's some sweet stuff there." Jamie cackled out a laugh.

Secretly, we'd all been jealous of Cohen's relationship. "Laugh it up, boys, but I've been there. The empty beds, broads each week, party after party. What do you think the seventies were like?"

"They would have rocked!" Ryan punched a two-handed rock-and-roll salute in the air.

Cohen rolled his eyes. "When I found her, I knew she was it. Thirty years later, we're still together." He switched off the mixing desk and turned to me. "Can you stay true to her and only her?"

My breath labored as I struggled to take in air. I stuck out my hand to steady myself.

"Kit, sit down. You don't look too good," Cohen said.

"Yes. It's crazy, but yes, I only want her. I only want Jazzie."

"Now, but how 'bout when the next Victoria's Secret model comes along?" Ryan asked.

I took longer and deeper breaths, everything becoming clearer after each second passed. "I've never wanted anyone as much as I want her."

"That's the spirit," Jamie said, slapping me across the shoulders and nearly sending me stumbling off my stool.

"But now what?" There was a big difference between me knowing I want Jazzie and her not wanting me.

"You leave that to me." Cohen grinned.

"No, Cohen." I patted his shoulder. "I have to figure this one out myself."

* * *

The warm glow of lanterns shone on the fresh canopy of snow in Central Park. I watched from my terrace as couples braved the cold just to stroll through the park with their other half. The oversized multi-million-dollar penthouse I'd bought two years ago was now feeling emptier than ever before.

I stared back at the architectural masterpiece like an outsider looking in. Expansive rooms, fitted out by the best interior design firm in Manhattan, with ridiculously high ceilings and large ten-foot windows. I had everything, but everything was nothing without her. I leaned on the iron balcony railing, casting my eyes down to the street. Even from up here, I could make out late-night lovers boating in the icy lake. This was the stuff that made me cringe. But now, more than ever, more than my career, fame, and fortune, I wanted to be one of those people.

I had to show her. I had to lay it all out. It was all or nothing. I reached for my phone in my back jeans pocket and hit the green call button.

"Kit?"

"Marcie, I need your help."

18

JASMINE

"She sees me through her lens
Like she doesn't pretend
Fire hair and green eyes,
I don't wanna say goodbye."

I gripped the steering wheel until my knuckles turned white. He'd written a song about me, and as much as it pained me to listen to the lyrics, there was no fucking way I could turn it off.

"Okay, spill the beans. For two weeks, you've been lying around the apartment like a bum. Jobless, miserable, and staring out the window like a zombie."

"Amber, come on, just leave it. Please."

I yanked the hand brake into position, nearly tearing the thing off, and slammed the car door shut. "Can we just have dinner and not talk about it?"

"Kit has written a song about you! You're crazy if you think we're not going to talk about what we just heard."

"Lily is probably waiting. Can we just go in?" I blinked back tears on the brink of completely falling apart. Keeping it all to myself, I hadn't told the girls about Kit and me—a dream I didn't want to wake up from. But keeping something like this from them was gnawing away at me. I thought I could forget and move on like I had so many times before. But this was different.

The time we spent together, I couldn't shake. Every moment, every heated gaze, and every electrifying touch was a constant reminder inked on my heart.

It was late on a Friday night when Amber dragged me out of our apartment. I'd missed our girlie catchup last week, too miserable to contemplate leaving my favorite sweats, a box of sugar-laden cereal, and my date with Netflix.

They packed into Sanders on the Bay. Full of twenty-somethings, it was a go-to restaurant and bar for singles who wanted a casual meal and the chance to meet someone who hopefully didn't have a Tinder profile. I glanced around the room for Lily, but all I found were people searching for love. I pushed down the emotion pooling in my throat. I was here, and I could at least put on a happy face. I had to try. Even if it was for a few hours, I owed it to myself.

"Right, there she is." Amber pointed.

I followed her direction, spotting Lily's blonde bob in the center of the room. "Let's go sit down, order a drink, then you better spill your guts."

I moaned out into the crowd of people, contemplating how to tell them about the surprise Kit turned out to be. Just thinking about it, I wanted to laugh. It was so absurd. So incredibly absurd. If I hadn't felt his lips on mine, I wouldn't even believe it to be true.

* * *

The chatter at the restaurant didn't dampen Lily's shriek when she spotted me approaching the table. Before I even sat down, she'd eyeballed me. "I just heard a snippet of Kit's new song. Jazzie, tell me that's not about you."

If only for a millisecond, anger coursed through me. After two weeks of hiding my funk, Kit had to ruin it all by releasing a song, making it even more real.

"It might be." I sighed, waiting for the barrage of questions to be unleashed.

"What the hell happened at that cottage?" Lily asked, dragging my hand down to sit.

As I sipped on my house wine, I pondered how to answer the question to my two best friends. The two besties I'd been through everything with. All the exes, the men who constantly disappointed me. All the heartache they'd helped me get through. Now, this. The shortest yet most authentic relationship I'd ever experienced.

"We're waiting." Amber tapped her pointy nails on the wooden table.

I sighed. "Let me preface by saying we were doomed from the start."

"Oh my God, you slept with him!" Lily burst out.

"I know, I don't have to tell you this, but what I'm about to say is between the three of us."

Amber and Lily immediately outstretched their arms into the center of the table, stacking their hands one on top of the other and waiting for me to do the same. It's a thing we did when we absolutely swore not to tell another living soul. There were a handful of secrets we'd shared over the years, and the vault we shared had some pretty sacred secrets.

I placed my hand atop theirs.

"Okay, it's in the vault. Now spill," Amber demanded.

"It started so innocently. It was just a job, one I didn't want to take initially. I didn't fawn after Kit like everyone else. But as the days progressed and the studio time got longer, I spent more time with him. It turned out he's just a normal guy with the kindest heart."

"But he's so smooth. So criminal with women," Lily said.

"Shut it, Lily. I want to hear all of this." Amber motioned for me to continue.

I laughed. Otherwise, the alternative was too sad. "So, we spent a lot of time together, just the two of us. And one time, we actually ran into my ex, and that's when he kissed me for the first time."

"Hang on. You saw Ajax, and then Kit kissed you? Did Ajax see?" Amber took her hands to her cheeks.

"Yes." I shivered, remembering how his lips felt on mine, his manly sandalwood scent I'd come to crave.

"Oh, my God, that's so cool. Suck on that, Ajax." Lily applauded.

A smile made its way onto my face, the first one in a while. "It was pretty cool, actually. Earlier, I'd told Kit about him and how I found him cheating. I guess he felt like he should protect me or prove a point to him."

Lily leaned forward, her elbows resting on the white tablecloth. "What was the kiss like?"

Heat scaled my neck. Describing a kiss with Kit was harder than lining up the perfect photo.

"Magical. Desperate. Passionate." I brushed my fingers along my lower lip, remembering every inch of his lips on mine.

The silence clawed me back to reality, and when I looked up, Amber's and Lily's eyes were on mine. "Anyway, so then he invited me to dinner at the house. He told me some stuff that was pretty real and made me realize a few things about myself."

"Like what?" Amber asked.

"Like maybe I should follow my passion, even though I've got the world stacked against me… my parents and sister. Maybe I should just try it, you know?"

"Is that why you quit your job?" Amber continued her line of questioning.

"Yes. It's part of the reason. I'd had enough of Fred putting me on all the shitty jobs, then promising the earth and not delivering. It's not where my passion lies."

"Okay, enough about work. What about Kit?" Lily pressed.

A server appeared at the table, and Lily's gaze fell upon his golden smile.

"Can I get you ladies another round?"

"No. Can't you tell we're in the middle of something?" Amber flapped her hand about in the air like she was swatting a swarm of bees, and he promptly left.

"Amber!" Lily yelled, her face flushed the color rose.

"You can get his number later," she hissed out.

She pouted her glossy lips. "He won't want my number after that."

"Go on, Jazzie," Amber said, ignoring her.

"So, the more time I spent with him, the more I didn't want to be apart from him. The physical attraction was off the charts too." I sipped my wine, trying to push away the memory of him between my thighs. I cleared my throat. "I just hadn't realized he was more than a pretty face. So then we caught a chopper to his parents' house."

"Shut the fuck up. You met his parents?" Lily squealed.

"I knew that one," Amber admitted. "But I thought it was all part of the job, nothing more."

"No, that was a date. His parents were so lovely. I can see how he's so grounded."

Amber and Lily exchanged glances. I guess hearing this for the first time would shock the toupee off a bald man, it was that unbelievable.

"Go on," Lily said.

"That was the first time he'd seen them for a long time. He had a lot of stuff to deal with since his brother died, then the memorial a few days later. He wanted me beside him, and to be honest, there was nowhere else I wanted to be. Even though I knew it was a bad idea, I just couldn't stay away."

"Are we at the juicy part yet?"

I tossed my hair behind my ear.

"Oh, hell yes, Lil, here it is." Amber laughed, and I couldn't help but laugh too.

"His parents have this boathouse. And oh my God…"

Amber grinned. "Does he have the Kit and Kaboodle?"

"Think of your best lover, then ten times that."

"Well, Hello Kitty," Lily exclaimed, and we all burst into laughter.

"Who would have thought Kit Jones would ever put a woman before his own needs." Surprise etched onto Amber's huge brown eyes.

"I know. But that's exactly Kit Jones and not just between the sheets."

"You lucky son-of-a bitch," Lily said wistfully.

Not anymore. The last thing I wanted to do was rehash my excruciating heartache.

I circled my fingers on the table, fidgeting with my thumbs. "He even asked me to move to New York with him. It was that perfect."

"What?" Lily and Amber both answered at the same time.

"But then it all fell apart. The day after he'd asked me, he called me wanting to meet early. I just guessed he wanted an answer." I shook my head. "That evening, I'd actually contemplated going to New York. Can you believe that?"

"Jazzie, why not? It's always what you wanted to do, travel the world taking photographs." Amber's voice became lighter, more excitable.

"Why not?" I bit out, my voice stern. "Maybe because he's becoming a dad? That kind of changes things now."

"Would you have moved if the baby wasn't in the picture?" Amber pressed.

I paused, the question stumping me. In the last two weeks of ruminating, I hadn't run that scenario.

I shrugged. "I don't know. Probably not."

"Because you fear being hurt again?" Amber asked.

I shrugged. Damn, she knew me too well. "I guess."

"But he found out about being a dad and still wanted you to move to New York with him?" Lily asked.

"Yeah, even then."

"And you said no because?" Amber stared at me like I'd grown a mustache.

"Because he has a child on the way, a tour, and an album, probably a whole heap of things that would keep us apart." I flicked my hair, annoyance running through my veins. "If that's not enough, every single boyfriend I've ever had has been disastrous."

Lily and Amber exchanged glances.

"You know what, guys, I don't expect you to understand. I just need simple, and I need easy. He's none of those things. In fact, he's the damn opposite. He is a worldwide star. I'm a photographer from Seaview without a job and a major disappointment to my parents."

"In your parents' eyes, you could never measure up to your sister's success, so why you even try, I don't know," Lily said.

"I'm over trying… I'm done. If I weren't done, I wouldn't have quit my job."

"Do they know you've quit?" Amber asked.

"Yes, I told them."

"I would have loved to have been a fly on the wall for that conversation." Amber tossed her brown hair over her shoulder.

"Yeah, it didn't go down well. They actually wanted me to go back to college or worse, take a job with Russell."

They both laughed, knowing me better than my own parents.

"But, what about Kit, Jazzie? Did you listen to the lyrics in the song?" Lily asked, her face laced with genuine concern.

"Of course, I did, but it doesn't change the fact I can't trust him."

"Has he given you a reason not to trust him?" Amber asked.

I thought about the time we spent together. Never once had Kit strayed from the truth.

"No, he hasn't. But look at who he is. He'll get sick of me, find someone else when he's done with his small-town fix… and me. I just couldn't handle that."

"I don't know, Jazzie. Maybe you should give the guy another chance," Lily said.

"I agree with Lily," Amber added. "Yes, it's inconvenient he's got a baby on the way, but he's not in love with her. It sounds like he's in love with you."

* * *

Amber knew not to say any more. She'd said enough at dinner. And even though I'd basically hijacked the entire dinner, I loved seeing Lil.

As I rounded the corner on our way home, I pretended to focus on the road, but the reality was I remained in my head. Shortly after we arrived home, I hid in my room, exhausted from all the questions and the emotional roller-coaster it sent me on.

I laid curled up on my bed in that semi-lucid state between sleep and consciousness. His enormous almond-shaped eyes stared into mine—his warm touch, so real on my skin. The warm taste of salt pulled me from my dream-like haze. A salty tear reminded me my dream was just that.

A dream.

With summer coming to an end, I needed to focus on a job, and get over him, stat.

A sadness filled my veins, threatening to take hold of me. Maybe I didn't want to get over Kit. I pushed it away, drifting into sleep.

* * *

Intrusive banging turned the warmth of my dreams into an instant nightmare.

"Wake up, Jazzie."

Her voice sounded louder by the second, and I squinted, realizing it wasn't a nightmare at all but Amber's annoying voice pounding the hollow-core door.

She fiddled with the handle, the brass knob rattling. "The damn door is stuck again!"

I groaned out. "Amber, leave me alone."

The loud bang of the door flying open arrowed me upright, sending the quilt flying.

Amber stood in the doorway, red-faced.

I rubbed my stinging eyes. "What time is it?"

She flung the sheets off me, and my body shivered. The warm cocoon of covers no longer kept my dreams about Kit intact. "Amber!" I yanked up the covers, trying to hold on to that feeling.

She plopped herself on my bed. "You need to see this." Her steely gaze piqued my curiosity.

"What is it?" I grabbed the phone she'd stuck a few inches from my face. Kit stared back at me from beyond the photo. Instantly, I'd recognized it as one of my own. It was my favorite photo of him. I quickly traced the headline, *Kit Reveals All in a Tell-All Interview.*

"What is this?" I asked Amber as I bit the side of my cheek.

"Read it. Read it aloud." The headline, along with the anticipation in her tone, was equal parts exhilarating and frightening. I swallowed. Nerves filled my body, but everything in me willed me to read it.

International rock sensation, Kit Jones, has been media fodder for international tabloids since he shot to fame in his band, Four Fingers, seven years ago. Now, it's his time to turn the tables. His time to set the record straight.

He did this interview with a fellow Aussie, Harry Stockdale, a journalist from the Brisbane Times *whom he met during his time in Australia.*

I gasped. "He did what?"

"Go on, Jazzie."

. . .

Harry: *Thanks for speaking with me, Kit. Just to be clear, nothing is off the table?*

Kit: *Nothing, Harry, but I'm guessing you're probably not too focused on my shoe size.*

Harry: *You guessed right, there. Okay, let's start with the baby news. You're going to be a dad. Can you tell us about the mother-to-be and what your thoughts are on the impending birth?*

Kit: *I met Carmel at a party before I came to Australia. We slept together, and when I was in Australia, she told me she was pregnant if only a few weeks. I was shocked but wanted to be there and protect my unborn baby. Without a doubt, Carmel knows I'll be there for our child, but she also knows there is nothing between us.*

Harry: *It's been one year since Drew's death. Understandably, his suicide rocked you. How has this really affected you?*

Kit: *Drew was everything to me. When he ended his life, it literally brought me to my knees. No one could comprehend what I went through. I guess you saw a lot in the headlines, but dulling the pain only ended up exacerbating it. I'm at peace now. I tried to help him, but he had his demons. I'm in the motions to set up a charity in his honor and to help other victims of mental illness. It's a battle no one should have to fight alone.*

Harry: *When you talk about dulling the pain, are you talking about women? The headlines speak about your countless forays with women. Is that an addiction?*

Kit: *(Laughs) I mean, I guess I kind of dulled my pain with women. No disrespect to them whatsoever, but I sought comfort in women, and for a while, it helped. No, I wasn't a sex addict. But I can see now how destructive it was. No one picks up on your behavior. That's the sad part. Everyone is scared to stand up to you and call you out when you're famous. It's just seen as the rock-and-roll way.*

Harry: *And how about your stint in rehab?*

Kit: *Yeah, that was rough. I had a problem with alcohol in the immediate weeks after Drew's death. I'd never had a problem with abusing alcohol before that. It was just a rough time in my life. The* counselors at rehab gave me the tools and strategies I needed. They were amazing. I've never had a problem with alcohol since then. I can have the occasional drink and be fine.

Harry: *Can you tell us about the photos taken in Las Vegas recently of you hitting your drummer, Angus?*

Kit: *We got into an argument.*

Harry: *About?*

Kit: *He said something that pissed me off about not protecting someone I cared about. We're okay now. Shit happens, you know?*

Harry: *You came to Seaview to write an EP but ended up coming out with three new singles. Completely different from your other stuff. Can you tell us about that? Why the new stuff, and why now?*

Kit: *Yeah, I'm really proud of the three songs I wrote in Seaview. But I can't take all the credit for that. Someone there helped me. Someone changed me for the better, and she inspired me so much so that the lyrics just came naturally and more easily than anything else I'd ever written.*

Harry: *Can you tell us more about her?*

Kit: *I'd love to. Her name is Jasmine, and she is the most amazing photographer and an even better human being. And during my time in Australia, she changed me. She made me realize a few things about myself that I hadn't before. And, although she can't trust me, I trust her implicitly. She's like no one I've ever met. And I hope she knows how special she is to me. She always will be.*

Harry: *Are you in love with her?*

Kit: *Without a doubt.*

Harry: *Wow, women around the world are going to be saddened by that announcement. Why aren't you two together?*

Kit: *Because my life is different from hers. I asked her to come to New York, but she declined. I want her to take a leap of faith and be with me. She's been hurt before. I promised I wouldn't hurt her.*

Harry: *How can you make those promises?*

Kit: *When you know deep in your heart that you're meant to be with someone, you just know.*

. . .

The phone slipped out of my hands, falling onto the bed as tears streamed down my cheek. "No way…"

My entire body shook, my hand trembling so much I gripped the edge of the bed to make it stop.

"Jazzie, say something." Amber put her hand on top of mine. But as my eyes blurred with tears, I couldn't find any words to comprehend what I'd just read.

Amber's hands landed on my shoulders as she shook me. "Jasmine, the guy has basically declared his love for you to the world. What are you going to do about it?"

My breath labored as my world spun. There was only one thing I could do, the only thing that felt right. Everything else over the past two weeks had felt wrong. Pushing him away and trying to forget him stabbed like a dagger and left me in more excruciating pain.

"You know, maybe he is exactly what you need."

"He is, Amber. He is imperfectly my kind of perfect."

19

KIT

"**M**an, I love New York," Jamie said. "Did you feel the buzz out there?"

I took a towel to my brow, dabbing the beads of sweat. "Yeah, it's swell."

"Fuck, Kit, these songs sound insane out here," Ryan said, his mouth falling open.

We'd just played in Times Square on Valentine's Day, and it didn't get any bigger and better than this moment. The New Year's Eve ball drop was probably the only thing that came close. But when we played there a few years back on the last day of the year, it was a different vibe than now. Maybe I was different. *Who knows?*

Two days had passed since I'd done the interview with Harry. Syndicated worldwide, the interview blew up bigger than I'd expected—front page of the *Times*, *Variety*, *The Independent*, and *The Sun*, just to name a few. In Australia, Harry had become an overnight celebrity, which he took to like a rat to d-Con.

Yet, the only thing that had mattered hadn't happened.

Jazzie hadn't called or tried to reach out another way. *Any way.*

I'd left it all on the line, and it wasn't enough. But I had no regrets. I couldn't.

The small intimate crowd started chanting the band's name. *"Four Fingers! Four Fingers!"*

Jamie threw back his ice water and grabbed a towel, wiping the beads of sweat from his face. Although freezing out, under the stage lights, it felt like the middle of summer.

Ryan did the same but sucked back something alcoholic. Bourbon was the likely choice he'd kept hidden in his white mug from the caramel malt that wafted.

I looked over my shoulder to the side of the stage, spotting the powerful duo, Marcie and Joy, both grinning from ear to ear, extremely happy with themselves and rightly so. They'd pulled a public relations rabbit out of the bag yet again. Joy knew the new songs were on the verge of selling a gazillion records.

Sensing my mood didn't match hers or anyone else's on the team, Marcie's grin plateaued as she took me in. She could organize the media with the click of a finger, but she couldn't make someone love me.

No one could.

She knew the depth of my sadness. When I'd called her and asked her to arrange the interview with Harry, she pushed back. Questioning me to make sure it was exactly what I wanted. I knew she had my back, but I just had to do it. So, true to Marcie, she'd made it happen, and an hour later, Harry, the annoying little twat from Seaview, who crushed on my Jazzie, was on the phone for a tell-all scoop.

Ryan patted me on the back. "This is dope, Kit. Let's finish strong."

I exhaled. I didn't know what to expect from the interview. But the shred of hope I'd held out after the interview faded fast as each hour went by that she hadn't reached out.

I picked up my guitar and flung the strap over my shoulder.

"Let's do this." Knowing she didn't feel the same way, the last song would be the hardest to get through. I followed Ryan and Jamie, who walked out toward the stage. The night sky shone a milky gray from the neon billboards in Times Square. Media, celebrities, and industry bodies were the small crowd chanting the band's name—the lucky group invited to the intimate launch of the new songs.

I walked up to the mic stand. For the first time in forever, butterflies gnawed at my chest, and I cleared my throat. "This is the last song of the night. This is a special song to me. It's new. I wrote it in Seaview about a girl. It's called "Flaming Heart.""

Cheers and whistles echoed around the stage, and as I sat down on my bar stool and tilted my chin to meet the mic stand, I scanned the crowd, hoping to find a glimpse of my flaming heart.

I cleared my mind as I did before every song and inhaled.

Jamie counted down. "Three... two... one."

My fingers routinely started playing the chords on my guitar. I closed my eyes and let the words spill from me.

As I strummed the final chord, I opened my eyes to a sea of phones and spotlights as they swayed side to side like a lighthouse beacon.

All the energy and emotion escaped my body. I'd put everything into it, and it sounded sweeter than I could have ever imagined.

The crowd screamed and yelled. They cheered, chanted, and they wanted more, but it was all I could give them. "Thank you, New York, and Happy Valentine's Day."

I walked off the stage and down the three steps around the back. Marcie and Joy both hugged and kissed me. A few executives from the record label cheered me and told me how amazing the songs were.

Yeah, no shit.

After what felt like an eternity, I left the throng of people backstage and flung the door shut to my makeshift green room. I splashed bottled water on my face, the icy liquid bringing me back down to earth. I flopped into the armchair, placed my head in my hands, and ignored the buzzing of people just beyond the door.

Time had passed. I wasn't sure how much time when I heard a knock at the door.

20

JASMINE

I'd never left Australia before. I'd left Seaview on many assignments, taking pictures and exploring Australia's harsh landscape and stunning coastlines, but leaving on a whim, on a plane to New York, was so out of character. So absolutely absurd. But as the plane descended and the turbulence jolted me from side to side, I'd never been so scared yet so sure of something in my entire life.

The last day and a half were a whirlwind. After reading the interview Amber thrust at me in my half-asleep state, I'd somehow found my passport, headed to the airport with the last of my savings, and caught the last flight out to New York City.

"Please prepare for landing. Cabin crew, please take your seats."

I gripped the plastic seat handles and stared out of the window. As we floated across the Manhattan skyline, buildings shot up in the night sky like beacons of light.

The tiny island of Manhattan looked like a mega-structure of towers and grids. The Empire State Building lit up with Valentine's Day hearts and skyscrapers illuminated from the inside out.

After waiting in line, an usher hurried me to the yellow cab pulling up.

The driver leaned out, "Where to, Lass? Red?"

Lass? "Times Square," I said, biting the inside of my cheek.

That's where Harry had said he'd be. The cabbie unlocked the door, and I slid in the back.

I'd called Harry back after reading the interview. After all, he'd left five messages. I asked him about Kit's sincerity —even though I knew his answer. He'd assured me every single word Kit uttered was never spoken in a truer way or form. Everything he said was unaltered and unchanged, printed as it was spoken. "Kit said that if I ever spoke to you again, Jazzie, to tell you to live your passion. He said you'd know what he means."

"Can you please turn up the heat?" I asked—the vinyl seats providing no warmth to the freezing cold.

"Sure. So is this your first time in New York?"

"Yes, it is."

"Here for business or pleasure?"

"Both," I said, hoping that if Kit rejected me straight out, I'd at least be able to start my passion for photographing the world through my lens. I'd told Amber to find a new roommate, and as crazy as it seemed, I didn't have a backup plan. I just knew with my camera, the thousands of photos I'd built up over my photography career and the New York landscape, I'd be okay. That's not to say my dad thought I was crazy.

The cabbie's phone buzzed, reminding me I hadn't checked mine since landing.

I turned it on, and after a few seconds, a few beeps came through.

When my parents had heard about the interview, they were as confused as my sister. Apart from the obvious, why-do-you-always-choose-the-wrong-guy concerns, they weren't as angry as I thought they'd be. Maybe because they knew they couldn't stop me.

I fired the same text off to Dad and Amber.

Me: *Just landed. I'll call you later x*

I put my phone in my duffle bag and watched the scenery change as we moved away from the airport toward the highway. Scores of cars flew by, and as I nestled into my seat and closed my eyes, I heard *him*.

It was only for a brief second, but his voice was unmistakably Kit's. "Stop. Can you go back?" I said to the cabbie, who fiddled with the radio dial.

"You're not another fan, are you? The world has gone nuts over Four Fingers."

A calm washed over me as his voice reverberated through the speakers in the back. "I'm a big fan." I felt myself heating from the neck up.

"Hang on, is this their live acoustic set? There were billboards everywhere about the show tonight."

"Yes. Can you step on it, please? I really need to make it before they finish." I stared at my watch, and it was after ten. If the plane hadn't been delayed, I'd be there already.

"You got it."

I slunk back into my seat and let his voice wash over me. Every sense coming alive, even in my deliriously tired state, he had this effect on me. I just hoped he'd be there when I arrived because I didn't have a plan B.

We hit a few bumps as he exited the bridge and

rounded the bend, pulling to a halt as the lights changed from amber to red. "Not long now," he said.

Applause and cheers filled the cab. Kit's smooth voice sounded so crystal clear, he could've been singing it in the shell of my ear.

"This is the last song of the night. This is a special song to me. I wrote it in Seaview. It's called "Flaming Heart.""

I jolted upright.

"You all right, miss?"

"Shush, please."

The cabbie glared at me in the rearview mirror. "Groupie," he muttered under his breath, and the biggest grin spread into my cheeks.

"I can't get any closer, luv." The cab pulled to a stop—hundreds, if not thousands, of people crammed between billboards and buildings. I looked through the windshield, barely making out a stage in front of people and barricades.

Quickly, I paid the cab driver and grabbed my duffle bag, then shut the door behind me.

The song finished playing in the cab only five minutes ago. *He had to still be here.*

Kit had written a song about me, about us, and it was a masterpiece.

I ran, my legs suddenly becoming alive after a twenty-one-hour flight. I didn't know where I was running, but heading for the stage seemed logical. Shuffling through slowly dispersing crowds, I sideswiped people hearing accents from all parts of the world and stopping when I reached a barricade.

"Show's over," a pretty girl said, taking me in.

I sucked in a breath, ignoring her. I moved beyond the barricade. *He has to be here.*

I traversed the throngs of people that were spreading

thin, making my way to the front until suddenly, I was stopped by security.

"Where do you think you're going?" His All-American accent stopped me from climbing the gate.

I must have looked like a crazed fan or serial-killer stalker, but I pushed that aside.

"I'm a friend of Kit's," I said with all the Australian polish I could muster after running three blocks.

"You and me both, sweetheart. But I can't let you through."

"I know how it sounds, but you don't understand. I really am."

"Move along." He ushered me away with his hand.

There was no way fucking security would stop me now. Not after I traveled halfway around the world.

"Now listen here." My voice grew noticeably louder. "I am Jasmine Winters. The song Kit wrote was about me. Now, if you don't let me through, I'll make sure you never run security detail again!"

Whoa. Where had that come from?

He started at me but didn't say a word.

I heard my pulse in my ear pounding louder and louder.

"Excuse me?" A woman standing near the demountable building approached me. Her gaze fell to my face, then my hair. "Shit, you are *her*... Jasmine?"

"Yes." I steeled, clearing my throat.

"Red hair and all." She smiled.

"Can I see Kit?"

Her face fell. "He just left."

21

KIT

The hot shower needles melted away the buzz of Times Square. I rested my head against the cool marble tiles, missing her like crazy. Suddenly, the sound of chimes filled the bathroom speakers.

What the fuck? Now, really? I stepped around the floor-to-ceiling glass and pressed the button. "Yes?"

"Mr. Jones, I have Marcie here to see you."

Seriously? What more could she possibly want to discuss tonight? I'd just performed my ass off and was literally spent. The last thing I wanted to talk about was my image. I sighed.

"Let her up." I clicked off the shower and reached for the heated towel.

Dabbing the beads of water off my chest and legs, I walked over to my oak dresser, pulling out my Calvins.

I heard the soft ding of the elevator from my bedroom. Hurriedly, I struggled to pull my jeans up my damp legs. "I'll be right there, Marcie."

I walked out of my bedroom barefoot, shirtless, with

towel draped around my neck, my jeans still clinging to my legs. "Hey, Marce…" I glanced up, then paused.

Jazzie stood just steps away from the elevator. The only thing between us was the round table bursting with orchids. Her red hair windswept around her arms as she clutched an overnight bag. Her eyes were puffy and her cheeks red from the chill, but she hadn't looked more beautiful than right now.

My pulse quickened, and I had the urge to run and pick her up. But something in her eyes warned me to stay where I was.

"Is it true, Chris?"

I gripped the towel around my neck, anchoring me into place and ensuring I didn't take another step toward her. "The interview and the lyrics? It's all true."

Her shoulders lowered as she exhaled.

Slowly and carefully, I stepped toward her. She remained rooted to the tile square she was standing on and clutched her bag tightly in her hands. I put one hand on hers. It felt clammy and tight.

Brown eyes to green, I willed her to let me in.

She sucked in a breath and slowly released the grasp she had around her bag. I placed it on the floor, my hand quickly returning to hers as it trembled beneath mine—her vulnerability alluringly beautiful.

"Everything I said is true. I don't want to be in a life where you're not in it with me, Jazzie."

She looked down, and I tilted her chin so she had no other choice but to face me.

"All this other stuff going on doesn't matter. The fame, the money, all of it. It doesn't make a shred of sense if you're not with me, by my side."

A smile crept onto her cheeks.

"You challenged me to be the best version of myself. I

can be the man you want me to be, Jazzie. I just need you to take a chance… please."

She blinked a few times. "Ask me the question, Chris."

I swallowed, knowing in this moment she could destroy my heart forever. I held both her hands in mine and took in a mountainous breath.

"Do you trust me, Jazzie?"

Her eyes brimmed with unshed tears. "Yes, Chris. I've completely fallen for you. You're everything that I shouldn't want but everything I need."

My body lightened as she squeezed my hands.

"I love you, Christopher Jones."

I wiped away the tear that slid down her cheek.

"I'm scared. So scared. But Chris, I trust you with my whole heart."

"I promise I will never hurt you, only always love you. I'm sorry to say you're stuck with me, red."

She smiled, and I took her head between my hands, kissing her with every fiber in me.

Knowing I was already the man she needed me to be.

Knowing the day I stopped putting her first was the day I died.

EPILOGUE
LILY

I snuck out of the Karaoke club.

I couldn't be here anymore.

They'd understand.

Jazzie and Amber belted out, rather boisterously, a Karaoke classic YMCA, actions included, and I couldn't help but laugh aloud as I slipped out the exit. My best friends weren't alone. They had the golden tones of Kit Jones, an international rockstar from the band, Four Fingers and Jasmine's boyfriend.

By the time they noticed me gone, I'd be halfway to the address that burned a hole in my pocket.

I glanced over my shoulder as I exited the building. As grateful as I was that Kit

flew us over to see Jazzie, watching them together turned my stomach into knots. Don't get me wrong. I was happy beyond words for Jazzie, but the tender look that swirled between them reminded me of my pain. Pain buried so deep. Otherwise, it threatened to ruin my entire existence.

Once upon a time, I was the single most important person to Blake Carter. Or so I thought.

He was the boy next door. My best friend turned lover.

I stepped onto the sidewalk and hailed a cab. It jerked to a sudden stop in front of me and I climbed inside.

"Where to, miss?"

"Corner of Lexington and East 65th Street."

The car lurched forward and my hands fell into my lap, clammy and warm. I fidgeted uncontrollably.

No backing out now, Lily.

In a short ride, I would be face to face with the boy I had loved. The boy that took my virginity six years ago, leaving without so much as a goodbye.

ALSO BY MISSY WALKER

SLATER SIBLINGS SERIES

Hungry Heart

Chained Heart

Iron Heart

ELITE MEN OF MANHATTAN SERIES

Forbidden Lust*

Forbidden Love*

Lost Love

Missing Love

Guarded Love

SMALL TOWN DESIRES SERIES

Trusting the Rockstar

Trusting the Ex

Trusting the Player

*Forbidden Lust/Love are a duet and to be read in order. All other books are
stand alones.*

Join Missy's Club

Hear about exclusive book releases, teasers, discounts and
book bundles before anyone else.

Sign up to Missy's newsletter here:
www.authormissywalker.com

Become part of Missy's Private Facebook Group where we
chat all things books, releases and of course fun giveaways!

https://www.facebook.com/groups/
missywalkersbookbabes

ACKNOWLEDGMENTS

Let's keep it brief because really, who wants to hear about a bunch of people you don't know?!

My biggest fan, my mum Maria. I don't know how you read the sex scenes I write, but you do, every single scene in every single book. Your advice and support are immeasurable.

Tanya, your critiques are so spot on and meticulous, gosh one would think you've got a Phd!

To my beta readers, Jen and Tori. I just couldn't do without you both.

And for my fans who keep showing up time and time again, wanting to read my books. I'm so truly humbled. I get to do what I want every day because of your support, so thank you.

I will continue to write romance books that are an escape from reality with characters you can fall in love with, just like I do.

Missy xx

ABOUT THE AUTHOR

Missy is an Australian author who writes kissing books with equal parts angst and steam. Stories about billionaires, forbidden romance, and second chances roll around in her mind probably more than they ought to.

When she's not writing, she's taking care of her two daughters and doting husband and conjuring up her next saucy plot.

Inspired by the acreage she lives on, Missy regularly distracts herself by visiting her orchard, baking naughty but delicious foods, and socialising with her girl squad.

Then there's her overweight cat Charlie, chickens, rabbit and bees if she needed another excuse to pass the time.

If you like Missy Walker's books, consider leaving a review on Amazon and Goodreads, and following her here:

tiktok.com/@authormissywalker
instagram.com/missywalkerauthor
facebook.com/AuthorMissyWalker
www.amazon.com/Missy-Walker
bookbub.com/profile/missy-walker

SNEAK PEAK INTO THE ELITE MEN OF MANHATTAN SERIES

FORBIDDEN LUST - A FORBIDDEN, BROTHERS BEST FRIEND STEAMY ROMANCE

Lourde

I had the name of a porn star—Lourde Diamond—seriously, Mom and Dad, thanks a lot.

The only difference between me and said porn star was my bank balance.

We were wealthy. Well, my family was rich—old money. My dad, like his daddy and his daddy before him, were media moguls, owning the greatest media empire in

North America. Their wives were hand-picked from note-worthy families and perfectly curated—primed, aristo-cratic, well-mannered, and relentless in playing their part and owning their duty. At eighteen, that's where my life was headed. It was abundantly clear by dearest Momma, being the perfect wife was an achievement one must uphold. Since maids helped me learn to walk, they had groomed me for the day when it would be my turn to become a wife. Etiquette, posture, finishing school, every other class, you name it, I'd done it.

Perfect in every part. I was waiting to be introduced to the perfect partner from a prestigious family, of course. Old money, preferably, as Momma would say. Did I tell you it was the twenty-first century? Fuck, you'd be correct for thinking we were in the fifties. You'd also be right in assuming I was getting bored with my life, bored with being prim and proper and what society expected of me.

After I slid the white satin glove down my forearm, then the next, I rested them on the ivory tulle of my balloon skirt. Next, I slid the tray of canapes closer. Popping one into my mouth, I swallowed the buttery salmon with horseradish cream on a thin wafer. Then picked up another, my tummy growling satisfactorily at the intake of food.

With my best friends, Pepper and Grace, I'd just finished my debutante ball. It was by invitation extended to high-society Manhattan, a tradition my mother wanted to uphold, regardless of my months of objections. *Who wants to celebrate the coming out of a young girl into a woman?*

News flash—I'd become a woman a few months ago when Josh took my V-card.

Now we were back at the sprawling penthouse on Park Avenue where I live with my parents, celebrating with a sprinkle of friends, but mostly Daddy's esteemed guests. I popped another canape in my mouth and glanced around. This wasn't a party for me, more like a gathering of Dad and Mom's favorite people.

With his perfectly groomed salt-and-pepper hair and tuxedo, Dad stood chatting with my boyfriend, Josh, and his parents. Josh, or Joshua, as Dad called him, is my boyfriend of three months. Introduced by our parents, Josh studied law at Cambridge and was following his parents' footsteps, who owned one of the oldest and prestigious law firms in Manhattan.

To the left, there was Momma, not a hair out of place with some other ladies of class in the Manhattan social circle. Next to her was my brother, Connor. He was conversing with his best friends, Barrett, Ari, and Magnus. With eight years between Connor and me, I wondered why they even had me at all. We looked nothing alike. I took after Dad with porcelain skin, hazel eyes, light brown hair, and high cheekbones, whereas Connor had Mom's striking blue eyes and blonde hair. The only thing we had in common was our height.

Connor looked over and raised his glass of champagne. I smiled. Then Barrett turned toward me and ever so slightly tipped his mouth into a smile. His stare from across the room pulled my breath into my throat.

I can't help it.

I still had a stupid crush on Barrett. Green eyes and dark brown almost black hair. He wasn't a boy. He was a man with broad shoulders, golden-colored muscles, and confidence in spades. A completely off-limits older man with fuck-all interest in his best friend's baby sister.

Barrett helped broker a deal for a brownstone in Brooklyn for my family. But Connor struck a friendship with Barrett, encouraging Barrett to go out and establish his own construction and development company—just completing his first boutique hotel renovation in Soho.

So what if I made a point to search social media to see who was on his arm this week. I wasn't a creep. Just curious was all. The man was like a vault. I knew this because my parents regularly invited him over for dinner when Connor came around, yet he was the most mysterious man ever.

"There you are," Josh said, pulling me away from my stupid one-sided crush. Instantly, guilt washed over me.

"Here I am." I smiled up at him, then grabbed another canape.

"Have you eaten all these?" He laughed, then pushed the tray away from me and toward the middle of the table.

Quickly, I glanced back at Barrett, but he was engrossed in conversation with the boys.

Ugh.

"I wish we could go now. This party is lame. I don't even get the whole debutante thing. I'm coming out to society. Where was I before?"

He raised a brow. "Don't be like that. It's tradition. Also, an excellent opportunity to meet people and network."

I don't need to network.

Josh looked past me and smiled at a man who slowed down near us.

"Senator, how nice to see you here," Josh said.

"Joshua, what are you doing here?"

"This is my girlfriend, Lourde Diamond."

God, it sounded worse than *Debbie Does Dallas.*

"Senator Masele, nice to see you again." I stood up and greeted him.

"Lourde, hello, dear, and congratulations on making your debut."

I smiled and nodded.

"Of course, you two would know each other." Josh smiled, and I noticed his jaw tick.

"I didn't know you two were dating. What a match made in society heaven. Your mother must be thrilled, Lourde."

"Ecstatic." I smiled sweetly.

He looked at me sideways, unsure if my answer was caked in sarcasm. It was.

After another boring hour of networking—as Josh aptly named it—we had arrived downtown. Seated in a private section of a club, Pepper and Grace sat beside me, sipping on bubbles, while Connor and Barrett sat opposite with dates who appeared like magnets when we arrived.

"This is so much better. Thanks for organizing, Connor," I said above the booming bass.

He took his attention from the woman whispering something in his ear. "No problem, sis, it's a big day for you."

I smiled, my gaze settling on Barrett and his date. I wish they weren't here—the women—that is. But if I had my boyfriend here, what was the big deal if they had company?

I looked around the club. *Where was Josh exactly?*

"So, what are your plans now? You're a woman and all." The way the word 'woman' rolled off Barrett's tongue made my thighs clench together.

Stop it, Lourde.

Your boyfriend was probably hurling over the toilet from the bottle of champagne he downed, and you're drooling over your silly man-crush.

I pushed away my wavy hair. "I'm thinking about helping with the family business."

Barrett smiled, and fuck, there went my ovaries. At the

same time, my brother choked on his whiskey, and reluctantly, I peeled my eyes away from Barrett. The Ms. Universe lookalike seated next to him rubbed him on the back, soft enough to do absolutely nothing. He didn't thank her. Instead, he looked up at me. "Since when, sis?"

"I've been thinking about it for a while. Maybe I could be an editor for a design magazine?"

He rolled his eyes. "None of the women in the Diamond family have ever worked, Lourde, and it's not starting now."

Barrett turned to my brother, arching a dark brow, but he said nothing. If he was surprised, he didn't voice it.

Walls felt as though they were closing in around my chest. "We're not in 1950 anymore!"

Pepper and Grace stopped their conversation and turned toward me.

"Sis," Connor said.

"Maybe we should dance?" Pepper squeezed my hand from under the table.

"Yes!" Grace had already shuffled out of the booth before I'd responded. Deciding I was sick of this discussion, I slid out after Pepper.

I swayed my hips on the dance floor. Then, sliding my hands down my ruby red dress that gripped my body, I closed my eyes and let the beat overcome me. Or perhaps it was the two glasses of bubbles I quickly downed. Whatever, I didn't care. I felt free.

After a while, I opened my eyes, my gaze settling on our table. Barrett's green eyes stared back at me. My cheeks burned cherry red while my skin heated all over. Thank God it was dark.

"Hey, where's Josh?"

I blinked a few times, then turned to Grace, who was looking at me curiously.

"B… bathroom," I managed to get out, and when I glanced back at Barrett, his lady friend had her hands around his neck.

Did I just imagine the whole thing? Ugh.

"Actually, I might check," I said to the girls who were dancing to "Unapologetic Bitch" by Madonna. Josh had said he was going to the toilet but had been gone for a while.

On the way to the bathroom, I bumped into Magnus and asked if he could check if Josh was, in fact, keeled over in the men's bathroom. After he came out, he informed me Josh wasn't there.

What the hell. I didn't know at this point if I was more aggravated over my brother's sexist comment, Barret for giving me that spine-tingling stare, or my missing boyfriend. And tonight was meant to be about me?

Finally, I gave up scouring the crowd and slipped out the back exit in need of some quiet. Outside, the air was brutally cold—the wind whipping down the sidewalk, tossing my hair around my shoulders. The music lowered to a dull thud, giving me the space to hear my own thoughts. Moans pulled my attention, and curiously I walked toward the sound.

I turned the corner.

No.

A girl with a tacky pleather skirt and a blonde bob was on her knees with Josh's dick in her mouth. "What the fuck, Josh?"

His eyes enlarged to the size of saucepans. "Oh, shit." He tried to zip up and push her aside, but I was already running away. I turned the corner and ran back toward the club. Nearly tripping over, I slammed into a chest and a scent so intoxicating, it momentarily pulled me away from my existence.

"Lourde?"

I stared up into his green eyes. It was Barrett, and I couldn't help it. My eyes spilled with tears.

"What happened? Do you want me to get your brother?" he asked.

I glared at him, fuming at the idea.

"Okay, not Connor. Just tell me what happened."

"I just saw my boyfriend getting a blow job in the alleyway."

"What the fuck?" His eyes darkened with rage. "I'll kill him," he said, his tone like ice.

"No, just take me home." I stared up at him, pleading.

He balled his fists by his sides.

"Please, Barrett." My voice came out on the verge of begging.

He put his arm around me, and we quickly walked in the opposite direction toward his car. In under ten minutes, we were back in front of 147 Park Avenue. Moments later, after sitting in silence, he turned to me.

"Hey, you okay?"

I kept my gaze down. I didn't want him to see my tear-stained cheeks and smeared mascara eyes. His fingers wrapped around my chin, tilting my face so I'd have no option but to face him.

"Don't think twice about him. You deserve so much better than that asshole."

His hands lingered on my chin, his thumb stroking my cheek.

"Of course, you're going to say that."

"What, why?" He removed his hand, but the warmth of his touch remained.

"You're just being kind. It's what everyone says to comfort someone. But what I really want to know is, why? What did I do to deserve *that?*"

"Nothing, you did absolutely nothing."

Sobs clogged my throat.

"Come here, Lourde."

He unclipped my seat belt, and with one deft move, lifted me over the center console and onto his lap, pulling me into his chest. Firm, broad muscles were everywhere, and his scent was a cocktail of manly things like tobacco, whiskey, and something forbidden.

When I wrapped my arms around his neck, his hands dipped lower around my waist. The air in the car grew thick. He was all I needed to forget. I glanced up, and his hooded eyes stared back. My heart thundered in my chest. "Will you make me forget?" I whisper.

I moved slightly closer, but he made no move to kiss me. Instead, he looked away and slid his hands from around my waist. "Lourde," he said, his voice like gravel.

"Just forget it, Barrett." I pulled the door latch open, stepped out as quickly as possible without splitting a side seam, and ran toward the glowing double doorways.

Fuck my life.

Continue reading Forbidden Lust at www.authormissywalker.com

www.ingramcontent.com/pod-product-compliance
Lightning Source LLC
Chambersburg PA
CBHW011602210726

48287CB00012BC/2722